Echo Across the Sands

M. A. Brown

Midnight Tide
PUBLISHING

CONTENT WARNING

Fantasy violence and gore, mention of child slavery and abuse, non-explicit sexual content including brief mention of former sexual assault related to a side character, attempted suicide and language.
This book is a dark fantasy romance. The relationships depicted are not intended to portray healthy partnerships.

For those who smile through
the pain that echos in their
heart.

Opal Isles
Nobleman's Palace
Fate's Downfall Crevice
Pyramid Mountains
Mines
Nobleman's House

The Sea of Callais
Harpie Isles
The Pits
Foundling House
Foundling Fountain
The Queen's Troth Tavern
The Pits
The City of Evernedi
N
E
S
Gypette

The World of the Travelers

In the beginning of the Travelers' universe, all things existed on one plain. But an evil arose, known simply as the Darkness.

The rest of creation had no choice but to take up arms against the Darkness to defend themselves against it and the horrible creatures it spawned. But the Darkness was winning, sweeping across the land in a terrifying tide. Until in some a spark was discovered, magic. Those with it formed a mighty counteroffensive, but the more magic they mastered and gained, so too did the Darkness. For an age the war waged, with catastrophic losses on both sides.

It was eventually concluded that if they couldn't beat the Darkness, they would trap it. In an event known as the Breaking, they shattered the world into Fragments to save it and raised walls around each remnant, trapping the Darkness in the spaces between. They then wove into existence the Void, a passage knitting all the broken pieces of the world together. They crafted doors with locks only they could open, and thus they became known as the Travelers.

Echo across the Sands takes place within the Travelers' universe in a Fragment known as Gypette, which has long been ruled by the descendants of one of the original Travelers who broke the world, Inana Ishtar.

Twenty-Two Years Ago

Her mother's death would not be a dignified one. Safiya knew this, had known it since the first moment she started slipping the Honey into her tea and into her wine. She'd expected it, but she had not quite expected *this*.

The Mad Queen, a moniker she earned long before the Honey began soaking into her mind, writhed about the room tearing at her dress, shredding the skirt into wisping gray ribbons eerily reminiscent of smoke from a funeral pyre. The courtiers looked on with pale faces not daring to whisper a word against her for fear that the queen in her state would order their heads severed from their bodies and placed on pikes to line the main causeways that led to the palace doors, like she'd done to so many others.

Her screams were a symphony, a desperate prayer sung to the Fate of Death, echoing around the high ceilings multiplying the sound and sending it back down to Safiya's horrified ears. She would have clapped her hands over them if it weren't undignified. She swallowed hard around the lump in her throat that she tried to tell herself wasn't guilt. As soon as she'd found the papers, had learned the depth of her mother's depravity, she knew what had to be done, whether the Fates ordained it or not. She could not let the thrashing monster before her continue her reign of terror. Safiya would spend the rest of her life atoning.

The queen's claws met flesh, and yet she did not stop as she fell to her knees, ripping, shredding, singing her dirge. Her movements slowed as though she moved through the very Honey that was the instrument of her downfall. Her breaths rattled, and her wails softened as she fell back onto her splayed wings in a puddle of crimson blood. Safiya watched her chest rise and lower, rise and lower until it ceased.

She stepped forward, the heel of her shoes clacking against the marble floor in a sound that was too loud in a room that was too still, too silent. The onlookers seemed to be holding their collective breaths, and Safiya wasn't entirely sure she wasn't holding hers as she reached her mother and knelt beside her.

Safiya brushed the loose onyx hairs off the queen's face and peered down at her. The sphynx before her was so many things. Her mother, her abuser, her queen. Safiya trailed her fingers down the Mad Queen's throat searching for a pulse, letting a small bit of her magic loose to skitter across the body to delve into her, just to make doubly sure that nothing beat within her chest. There was only silence. The blood beneath them changed in color, fading from red to the crushed velvety blue of night speckled with gilded stars, her magic leaving her body. It was always the last thing to leave, the color so similar to Safiya's own and yet so much darker. It smelled of bloody battles, of crashing waves, of the crush of the sea and the desert at sundown.

For show, or maybe for herself, she pressed a kiss to her mother's blood-smeared brow, her lips coming away scarlet and tasting of her mother's iron-will brought down and ground into dust. She wrapped her hands around the crown, its aureate tips like the points of blades from which her mother's magic dripped, and stood raising it above her head. "The queen is dead." Her voice thundered across the room, and as though her words broke a spell, everyone started to whisper. She wasn't sure who moved first, if it even mattered, but one by one the assembled began to kneel, their hands pressed over their hearts, their wings tucked in deference.

"Long live the Queen! Long live the Queen! Long live the Queen!" The chant filled the room as the nobles loudly proclaimed their fealty, but already in the shadows she could see the council members circling like the carrion that they were, scheming how best to usurp or puppet her. Her knuckles turned white on the crown, its jagged edges cutting into her palm as she lowered it and strode from the room, leaving her mother's corpse behind, determination written plainly across her features. She would be damned if she let them get the better of her.

Part
One

Chapter 1

The boy bit back a whimper, his blood and dirt-streaked face hidden behind his small fingers. He huddled in the dank corner of the covered cart wrapped thinly in threadbare sackcloth. His golden eyes were rimmed red from days of crying. His shoulders still trembled in silent dry sobs. There were other children there, but none of them spoke either, though he was distantly aware that they looked as hollowed out as he felt. He could not remember his last meal or his last drink. His lips cracked, and his nostrils burned with the stench of all their bodies pressed together for too long.

He turned his head away from the dismal sight and rested his forehead against the rough wall of the cart. He picked at a splinter absently until it fell free and stuck in his thumb and bled. He stuck it into his mouth and sucked on it until all he could taste was the metallic salt of it. He kept it there until it no longer throbbed, and then he kept it there because it soothed him like he thought it might have once upon a time when he was still loved. His memories of love had gone stiff like his parents' corpses; they were there, but they were empty, a faded and distant recollection that he wasn't sure he hadn't dreamt to comfort himself when the cold swept across the pitiless desert at night.

He started at the shouts of men; the bodies of the other children stirred around him, trying to put themselves as far away from cart doors as possible, mewling like lost kittens. The doors banged open, and thick talon-tipped hands grabbed at arms, legs, and feet and dragged him out. They shouted in a language he was only distantly familiar with and pulled him into the sun.

He staggered, blinking, blinded by the light as someone slipped a loop of scratchy rope around his neck and cinched it tight—not so tight he couldn't breathe, but tight enough he couldn't even dream of running. He stumbled, stubbing his toes, as someone on the other end tugged. As he trudged along, his vision returned blearily and begrudgingly. They were in some sort of camp. Trees stood thick and tall like a hoard of unfriendly soldiers around them; boulders covered in flaking green lichen littered the hillside. The air smelled foreign, saltless, and his throat constricted as he thought of how far from the sea they must be.

He and the other children were strung like caught fish along the same line, pulled by a sphynx brute in leathers. He barked orders and greetings to others around him as he yanked them along through the camp of canvas tents pitched on roughly hewn wood platforms. Fires burned here and there, some with blackened cook pots slung low over them. The savory smell of stew felt like a punch to his overly hungry gut.

The ragtag procession halted. He braced his hands on his knees, his lungs grasping for breaths that stayed too fleetingly. The short journey exhausted him, and his muscles screamed, protesting so much movement after what seemed like an eternity in the same cramped position. A sphynx female walked down from a place he couldn't see between the trees and began pacing the line, pausing to occasionally pinch, poke, prod, or ask short, clipped questions of the other children. A few of the girls and younger boys were hauled off, but he tried not to think of where.

The square-jawed woman with her head shorn grabbed him by the chin, her claws dimpling his skin. "You, boy, what is your name?"

He licked his cracked lips, he couldn't give her his first name, someone might know that one, even here, so he gave her his middle. It came out little better than a rasp. "Oci . . . Ocidynus."

"Do you know why you are here, Ocidynus?"

His eyes tried to well up with tears, and he shook his head, his matted hair tumbling in front of his face.

The sphynx righted herself and cracked her voice like a whip over the lot of them left. "The good Queen Freylinn, long may she reign, has taken control of your lands and *property. But she is generous, she spared you, and as you are now orphans, you are all now wards of the crown. As such, you will work off your care debt to her in the mines. Should you survive until the time you come of age, you will be given the opportunity to join the army for training." She gestured behind her to the ramshackle camp. "This is your home now. Do you understand?"*

There was a dejected shuffling of feet and sniffling in answer. Tools were shoved into quivering hands, then Ocidynus and the other children were led, stumbling, by the string through the trees to the gaping maw of the mines. Into the belly of a beast they were dragged, uncertain if they would ever come out again.

Ocidynus woke with a start as the wagon he rode in lurched. He swabbed sweat from his brow and shoved the memories he dreamt of back. They always surfaced when he had to ride any distance in a wagon, carriage, or cart. A reminder to stay the course even though the mine was years behind him.

He lifted aside the canvas flap of the army cart. In the distance, the spires of Evernedi stood needle sharp, spearing into the sky, narrow towers with spiral stairs to nowhere, places of prayer where people would go to sing their blessings and woes to the Fates. Oci spat, the Fates be damned, and shifted his large membranous wings to sit more comfortably on the cart bench. He couldn't wait to don his new leathers, as these ones pinched where they were carved out around the base of his wings, having been designed for sphynx rather than valkry like himself. He'd had the ones in his trunk made especially for the Trials; he had to look his best if he was to win the position of the queen's bonded guard. Only two among them would be chosen, one for the queen and one for the princess, and he'd be damned if he had to be the one to babysit the little bitch.

Of course, the girl would need to pass the Ordeal in order for him to reach that next step, but he knew she would, he had been told, and those who did the telling were never wrong. He pulled his flask from where it was tucked behind his leather breastplate, popped the lid, and threw back some of the liqueur, letting it burn away the ghosts of his youth. He hissed as he recapped it and met the strange and sullen gaze of the Mutt, Abrax, across from him. The half-sphynx half-valkry bastard was nothing but a pup, he shouldn't have even been allowed to compete in the Trials, but with a dead mother and an absent father, or so the rumors said, there was no one to stop him. Oci pitied the poor bastard; perhaps he saw a bit of himself in the young man, or perhaps he had a soft spot for orphans, only the Fates could say.

He passed the flask over. "To the Fates who fucked us and the women we'll fuck, eh, Mutt?"

The Mutt's lip curled, showing one slight fang, and he shook his head but grabbed the flask and took a deep drag off it anyhow. "I have a name, Oci."

Oci chuckled darkly and pointed in the direction they headed. "Not to them you don't."

Chapter 2

The prismatic rainbows fractured across Xandrina's floor, dancing in the light of the early morning sun. Her lady's maid had not come that morning as was tradition, as she was meant to be spending the hours before her ordeal readying herself in quiet contemplation. She typically preferred quiet to her lady's nattering, but this sort didn't suit her. It was too heavy, filled with the dense weight of expectations and anticipation.

She threw her thin coverlet off, it was already stifling in the room despite the early hour, and stalked in her chemise to her balcony doors, the tips of her wings trailing along the floor behind her painted with the rainbow light. She threw the doors open, letting the boisterous riot of sound in with the slight breeze. She strode to the railing and leaned over, the wind teasing the ends of her copper waves into a tempest. All through the courtyards below and out into the city people were bustling to get their work done in preparation for her Ordeal, but most importantly for the ball and Trial that would come after to celebrate her should she succeed. Giddy flutters swooped and swarmed in her stomach at the thought. Days of tournaments, drinking, dancing, and gorgeous gowns.

But more importantly, she would finally be declared the heir. The statue of Glendora the Graceful moved out of the corner of her eye, coming from the shadows of its alcove to rest a stony hand upon her shoulder. The castle was haunted by the ghosts of queens past, not all —her infamous grandmother was not among them—but most, and they often took to possessing the statues littered around the keep. Glendora had taken to wandering in and out of Xandrina's rooms over the past few years, keeping a watchful eye on her, doing everything from letting Xandrina vent frustrations to being a waltz or sparring partner. The possessed statue couldn't speak, obviously, but there was a dancing finger language that they'd developed over the centuries to communicate with their living descendants, and besides that, there was a lot that could be said with facial expressions, even ones carved of marble.

"You're nervous, dear heart?" Glendora signed with her free hand; the smooth gray of her brow was bunched with worry.

Xandrina would never admit it to anyone else, not where her mother could hear and because she was supposed to be the picture of confidence—the throne could not waver for if it was seen to waver, the people might begin to think it could fall, and their line must never fall—but she was nervous. For all her training in combat and magic for all her hours of study, what if she failed? She would not only be failing herself and her mother, but she would be failing an entire country. There were no do-overs in the Ordeal; if she didn't succeed the first time, she would be exiled—if it didn't cost her her life. Her eyes darted around to make certain that they were truly alone, before she signed back swiftly, *"I am."* She didn't trust her voice not to falter should she speak the words aloud.

The statue's gaze softened somehow as Xandrina turned to face her, its hand sliding up to cup her cheek with its cool fingers, the touch tender and motherly, something her own Queen Mother was not allowed to be, as was the way with the sphynx royals. *"You will shine, dear heart. You were made to be an heir, a queen, I swear it."*

Xandrina smiled as the deceased queen's words soothed over the places within that had cracked with worry, healing them before they could fester into something darker and more debilitating. "I'd better get ready, then."

Chapter 3

Safiya's seat dug into the backs of her thighs as she perched on its edge. The magic in every stone of the sacred Trial Grounds danced along her bones, singing its greeting to the magic that lay within her. It hummed remembrances of her own ordeal, a harmony of horrors that it plucked from the darkest recesses of her mind for her to fight, as was tradition. The practice was meant to hew the weakness from the potential heirs, carving them down until there was nothing left but the strength needed for them to rule. Safiya flinched, fighting back the memories, putting them in their place as they threatened to overwhelm her. She'd been so young, so much younger than was typically allowed, so much younger than Xandrina, whom she could picture pacing in the waiting room on the other end of the dark tunnel that led out onto the stadium's sandy floor. She tapped her claw along the arm of her chair three times, once for every year older her daughter was than she was in the same position. Safiya tapped again, three extra years to hone her fighting and magic. Xandrina would come out of it just fine, Safiya was sure, but she soundlessly moved her lips in a short prayer to the Fates of life and battle, just to be sure.

On the rises surrounding her royal box, every dignitary and noble family from even the farthest corners of Gypette stood eagerly waiting, wings bunched tightly at their backs. Merchants wealthy enough to afford tickets held their children aloft on their shoulders so they could better witness this once-in-a-lifetime spectacle. Not that the princess would see any of it from her vantage below. A blanket of obscuring magic hovered above the fighting field, leaving the would-be heir in isolation for her task while allowing those watching to see her clearly as though they looked upon her through glass. The enchantment also worked to magnify and project the whole of the Ordeal upon magically imbued glasses that hung outside of the colosseum for the commoners to congregate beneath and watch, valuable relics left from the time of the Breaking that no Traveler since had been able to replicate. They were only brought out for occasions of import such as this.

Her gaze cut across the arena- snagged on the reflection of sun against silver armor at the mouth of the tunnel a hair's breadth before the spectators saw her. Xandrina stepped forward in skirts divided for fighting, her sword slung along her spine, the hilt peeking out from between her wings. Safiya's breath caught as the ends of her daughter's hair lifted ethereally in a breeze, and her claw-tipped fingers, stained with the colors of the cosmos, flexed at her side, not with nerves but with the itch of waiting power that Safiya knew so well. Her heartbeat swelled against her ribs with pride in every pulse; her daughter was everything an heir should be.

The roar of the assembled whipped like a tempest wind as Xandrina drew her sword and let her magic flow free, dark flames shimmering across the blade. A tremor shook the stones. The sand rippled in waves across the arena floor as a pedestal topped with the legendary scepter of Orinda rose from the center of the fighting field. From below its base, the magic imbued in the sacred ground began to birth beasts, their forms plucked from Xandrina's deepest fears. Fearsome things crafted of pure terror, talons, and tails. Some with scales and some with fur, they made an unholy racket as they surged toward her daughter.

Safiya blinked, and for a heart-stopping moment, she imagined in place of her fully grown daughter stood a fiery chubby-cheeked toddler holding her mother's sword, too big for her plump little hands with naught but wing buds on her back, tender and new and unable to help her flee from the nightmares in front of her. Magic tingled at the tips of Safiya's fingers as her claws lengthened. Her legs tensed as she prepared to launch herself into the air, to swoop down and scoop up her baby, to cradle her in her arms and fly her to a place without monsters, without ordeals or the burden of ruling a nation. But then she blinked again, and whatever spell memory had wrapped her mind in was ended.

The queen stilled, preternaturally, aware of every muscle in her body and every line of tension written across it. Slowly, casually, she leaned back into her chair and willed her whole being to relax bit by bit, keeping her eyes trained not on her daughter but at the ring of runes etched into the wall's rim above the fighting ground. This- this was why queens were meant to distance themselves from their offspring. Fates knows her mother was not an affectionate one, but that was never the sort of parent Safiya had wanted to be, and for the first years of her daughter's life, she hadn't been. She'd had a secret corridor constructed between her chambers and her daughter's rooms so she could slip in and snuggle Xandrina night after night, pressing her daughter's little body into the curve of her own and whispering fanciful stories into her hair as she fell asleep.

When Xandri was seven, all skinned knees, freckles, and smiles, someone made an attempt on her life for the first time, and Safiya knew then why queens were meant to distance themselves. Safiya knew that if it was she on that arena floor, it would not be the scepter of Orinda on that pedestal for her to retrieve but the memory of her prone daughter's wounded body, her blood spilling across the stones with harpie assassins, painted and dressed to blend into the shadows between them, rather than beasts for her to fight off.

After her little princess was healed all those years ago, Safiya sealed the passage between their rooms with a blood spell. The hurt in her sweet girl's eyes when she pushed her away for the first time would haunt Safiya until her dying breath. From that moment, and every moment afterward that she'd spurned her daughter's affection, a brick was placed between them, until now a wall of hurt was built so high and deep between them that Safiya didn't see a way it could possibly be torn down even if she wanted to risk Xandrina's safety.

Safiya applauded when the crowd around her surged from their seats with collective gasps followed by uproarious cheers, though she refused to look. Being seen to be indifferent was just as bad as being overtly affectionate, so she walked the razor-sharp edge of a headsman's axe with everything she did. It was no wonder her mother went mad, even before the Honey.

"She's doing better than anticipated, quite a fine specimen indeed." The queen gripped the arms of her chair as she battled the urge to physically recoil from the oily curl of her most senior councilman's voice as he leaned in.

She cleared her throat, forcing down a growl. Fayden, the bastard, was one of the last surviving relics of her mother's reign, a festering rot of a sphynx that had his roots burrowed so deep in the palace there was no pulling him out, not by force. She constantly had to maneuver her way around him, his stubbornly outdated ideals, his refusal to adapt, and his unyielding sense of superiority. She constantly had eyes on him, hoping, waiting for something, anything that could give her the leverage necessary to rip him from his position. Her web of whispers was spun through nearly every corner of the capital, comprising of sphynx in all walks of life from the most highly sought after courtesans to the most common prostitutes in the Pit's taverns, from merchant cooks to ladies' maids. Which was how her web discovered the sniveling man had bet against her daughter, making traitorous claims that the Traveler magic in her was all but completely diluted of its fire. The amount of money he placed on her daughter's demise had Safiya wishing she could go to the collection houses to watch him count the coins over personally, and now the greasy son of a harpie had the audacity to turn his coat and call her daughter a *fine specimen* as though she were no better than a prize beast at auction. "Yes, well, I'm glad to know she has your loyal support, councilman."

Though as she said it, she sent a silent prayer to any Fate who would listen that by the time her daughter needed to take the throne, the wrinkled old windbag would be long for the grave.

A trembling in the pulse of the magic around them drew her attention from Fayden and back to the center of the arena where the magical veil was pulled back, allowing her daughter to see the onlookers for the first time. She stood among the steaming remnants of a dozen or more Owlvyrn corpses, reduced to piles of scaly tales, fanged beaks, and feathered wings by the swing of Xandrina's blade.

Xandrina lifted her arms, the Scepter of Orinda in one hand, her sword in the other, and roared her victory to the sky with the ichor of the slain beasts dripping down her face. The crowd was on its feet, stomping, her name chanted like a war cry falling from their lips. Safiya stood with the rest of them and walked to the edge of her box to lean over its edge, her gaze locking with her daughter's. There was a question in Xandrina's eyes, and Safiya answered it with the barest nod of approval. Pride filled Safiya's heart, swelling it until it threatened to burst within the tight grip she held it in. Her daughter had won the right to be heir to the throne of Gypette.

Chapter 4

Xandrina's dress might have been made of golden starlight for all the glittering embroidery and near-sheer fabric that snugged around the sweetheart bodice and down the flowing layers of skirts. A gilt-scaled pauldron covered her left shoulder, and slung across her waist was a decorative belt with her ceremonial sword in its jeweled scabbard. The blade was blunt and useless, unlike the knives strapped to her thighs, and completely impractical. It was meant to be symbolic of the might of the throne more than anything else, and she looked forward to shucking it off as soon as she was crowned. There was no way she was going to cart its dead weight around all night.

The mistress of ceremonies buzzed around her like an anxious bee, fluffing her skirts, picking dust that wasn't there, and making sure the shimmering powder brushed across her skin was just right. "Perfect," she muttered as she went, "you look just perfect, Your Highness."

Xandrina sighed and rolled her eyes. She knew how she looked—as she should, like the warrior heiress to the throne—she didn't need or want nervous platitudes. She flicked her wrist, shooing the woman away, as she strode for the doors to the Great Hall. Their hinges groaned a greeting as they opened onto the sea of waiting nobles and visiting dignitaries, along with those who held no titles but were wealthy enough to buy their way in. They parted along the center of the room, leaving an empty aisle. Their heads swiveled round to stare as she squared her shoulders and took her first steps on the long walk to where her mother stood waiting in front of her throne on the dais.

The queen stood like an elegant storm, beautiful and deadly, the train of her gown spilling like blood off her hips and down the stairs, the rose-gold crown on her head spearing the air like dagger-tipped lightning. Her amber eyes shimmered with something like viscous pride as Xandrina bowed before her, reminiscent of the looks her mother had given her once upon a time when she was a small girl. But that was before, and the memories faded like the lines of an old fairytale. This was real and so much better.

The ancient words were intoned, though Xandrina could barely hear them over the hum of her magic as it surged through her blood, calling to the crown as it was placed reverently upon her head. The golden heir's circlet was heavier than she'd anticipated. It was a weight that settled not on her neck and shoulders but in her soul.

When she rose and took her place on the smaller throne next to her mother before the crowd for the first time, she saw not just a milling mass of sycophantic nobles, but *her people*, each soul tethered to the land and to the throne. To her and to her mother. She would someday hold the responsibility of each of their lives in her hands. She'd known this, had been raised knowing this, but now she felt it more sharply. A wave of nausea rolled through her, swelling and threatening to spill her meager lunch at her mother's feet. She would rather go through the Ordeal a dozen more times than feel this.

One at a time, people stepped forward, from councilmen with lecherous stares to merchants showing off their sons in hopes she might take an interest in them and offer them positions at court. She smiled, her mouth pulled tight, and nodded graciously at each in turn, politely thanking them for the gifts they left at the foot of the dais.

Her mother leaned against the arm of her throne close to brushing Xandrina's shoulder with hers, and whispered, her voice pitched so low it was only audible to her, "You get used to it."

Xandrina darted a glance at her mother, who sat statuesque save for her thumb that seemed to brush unconsciously over the scar that slanted across her lips, and asked, "What do you mean?"

"The burden of it. It doesn't get lighter; in fact, it's quite the opposite once you put on the queen's crown, but you get stronger. And then one day, it becomes less a burden and more a privilege."

She stared blatantly at her queen mother with a decidedly unprincesslike expression of awe on her face.

Her mother raised an eyebrow, and the hint of a small smile tugged at the corner of her lips. "What? Did you think my crowning was so long ago that I've forgotten what it felt like?"

A flush crept across Xandrina's cheeks as her mother chuckled softly. While she could still remember a time when her mother's laugh was unrestrained, those memories were hazy and tinged with the haze of time. This laugh was a shiny new treasure, one that held hope that maybe they could one day be close again. Her mother reached out and patted her cheek in a way Xandrina felt was meant to be tender. It was the barest of affections, but Xandrina soaked it up as if it were the noonday sun.

A servant at the foot of the dais broke the spell of the moment announcing the next dignitary in his sonorous tone, "The Scholar Cato hailing from Ifris."

Xandrina perked up in her seat, tilting toward its edge. Ifris was a distant Fragment, home to the Drakar people if she remembered her studies correctly, which could only mean . . . "You're a Traveler." Her words were sugarcoated with wonder as she took in the peculiar man before them. His skin was covered in emerald scales; his brilliant-yellow eyes were wide over a flat nose and full of the dust of old books and the wisdom gleaned from their pages. His purple robes hung to the floor, their edges trimmed in elegant, ornamental embroidery that, if she recalled correctly, indicated his rank among the scholars in the famed libraries of the Drakar, beneath which the end of a tail curled at his feet. On his belt hung a chain with small silver keys tarnished with age, for Traveling. It made her fingers itch and her magic sit up full of curiosity just to look at them.

The Drakar Cato lowered his hood to reveal twin horns that curled back away from his forehead as he swept into a bow. "I am, Your Highness, Your Majesty. I have traveled a long way to observe and record the ceremonies for posterity's sake."

"We are greatly honored that you have come all this way, Master Cato." Her mother shifted forward on the precipice between remaining seated and standing. "And might I say what a pleasure it is to see you again after all these years."

Joy crinkled the corners of the Drakar's eyes as they flashed with something like pride. "Ahh, I was wondering if you would remember me, Majesty."

"It's not been so long that I would forget." She turned to Xandrina. "Master Cato was here to document my own ordeal and crowning."

"And just as I did before, I come bearing gifts for the new heir." Cato motioned a servant Xandrina had not noticed waiting with a large iron box forward. The man struggled under the weight of it, and Xandrina craned her neck, torn between sweeping down the steps to get a closer look and remaining on her throne for dignity's sake.

With a flick of his glowing fingers, the lid of the small chest flipped open with only a slight protest from the hinges. After a moment of cooing and coaxing while Xandrina waited, curiosity cinching her lungs, Cato pulled a creature from its dark depths.

The beast had a feline shape to its head and forebody, but it lacked the amount of fur one could usually expect. It was instead covered in patterned, pearlescent purple scales from the base of its tufted ears to the rattle-tipped point of its snakelike hind body. Two glimmering fangs glinted as silver as a slivered moon as it slithered up the scholar's arm, pausing to hiss huffily in Cato's face, clearly not happy at having been confined, before it settled across the Traveler's shoulders. It licked its forepaw and ran it vainly over its ears and whiskers, before turning a squint-eyed glare on her and her mother.

Xandrina gasped. "That's not, it can't be . . ."

Cato beamed a smile showing off his pointed teeth. "Ah, but she is, Your Highness. A Tatzelwurm. Fiercely loyal, protective, a touch magical, and yours if you will have her."

The princess rose, only two decades of training kept poise and grace in her steps as she descended the stairs. The Tatzelwurm slithered from its perch to meet her on the floor, its tail coiling behind it like a whip. Xandrina crouched down, her skirts clouding around her, and held out a hand for the creature to sniff. Its slit pupils contracted suspiciously inside its star bright irises before it gave her a twitch of its whiskers and slunk up her arm. The Tatzelwurm settled on Xandrina's opposite shoulder, its long serpentine body draped across her back and coiled around the arm it had ascended like a bizarre and incredibly large piece of jewelry.

Cato clapped his hands before folding them atop the rotund swell of his pot belly. "Ah wonderful, she's accepted you. I knew she would; she has very discerning taste."

The Tatzelwurm butted her head against Xandrina's cheek with a low purr that peculiarly sounded a lot like the words, *Of course I do*, before settling back down.

Behind her the queen stood, gliding down the steps to stand next to her. If Xandrina wasn't mistaken, the queen looked pleased, which did fluttery things to her heart. "Cato, you have outdone yourself, what a lovely gift." She descended the final step to put a hand on his shoulder. "Come now, the feast will begin soon, and I would love to have you sit next to me and tell me all the news from the other Fragments and what's been going on in the Circle."

The Drakar blushed, his tail twitching almost bashfully at his feet. "Why, thank you, Your Majesty, I would be honored." He offered an elbow in a gentlemanly fashion, which her mother took.

Xandrina followed a gold-clad shadow in their wake down the corridor to the banquet hall, her feathers ruffling in anticipation. At the feast, the Trial's contestants would be presented, and she couldn't wait to see who was among them. One winner, of course, was competing to be her mother's personal guard, but one would be hers alone. Her bonded, her sole protector until one day she became queen. Her mother's bonded had died in some mysterious accident that no one was willing to talk about, not even the gossipiest of servants would crack their lips on the subject, before she ascended the throne. She was the first queen in Gypette history to ascend the throne without a one.

My name is Lyrahvi, not that you asked, princess. The Tatzelwurm's purred words caressed her mind, feeling faintly annoyed.

Xandrina's stride faltered for half a step. "Did you just -?"

Of course, you silly girl, and you don't have to speak out loud. People will think you're insane if you keep carrying on conversations with yourself, Lyrahvi crooned with self-assured mirth. *I've deemed you worthy enough to be my pet, so now we are connected, I can read your thoughts, and you can read mine. Well, when I let you.*

*I'm **your** pet?* Xandrina thought wryly.

A laugh like a hiss slithered through her mind. *Of course you are, silly girl, now stand straighter so I can see better and quit bumping me with your wings.*

The princess sighed but with the hint of a laugh tethered to its end and did as Lyrahvi asked as they entered the banquet hall and took their seats on the dais overlooking the room. Garlands of scarlet desert lily and gilded globemallow were expertly woven together in a tasseled tapestry across the ceiling with fringes of fragrant greens vining down the columns and over the heads of those feasting and dancing alike. The globes of sweetly scented gilded globemallow were emitting their signature luminescent aureate aura, casting golden halos across the floor. Behind her and her mother, the sun was setting through the prism-cut windows, painting their skin in rainbows, a very intentional effect meant to symbolize the Fates blessings upon them and their reign. The whole room was steeped gratuitously in opulence.

The four-course feast that commenced as soon as they took their seats progressed uneventfully. Xandrina fed a very demanding Lyrahvi bits of roasted wombellow and savory sauce from her plate while her mother conversed animatedly with Cato, who sat on her other side, about Traveler matters and other things Xandrina couldn't pick up on.

Once the last of the dessert plates had been cleared, fluted chalices of sparkling wine from the Opal Isles had been filled and refilled for several rounds of toasts to her mother's long and healthy reign and to her well-being and success. As the minstrels plucked their stringed instruments in a more jovial and upbeat tune, a lithe woman sang from the mezzanine, her voice rich and velvety floated across the heads of the those who danced, their skirts fluttering in the night breeze that wafted from the open windows like the wings of the iridescent hummingbirds that liked to frequent the morning gardens.

It wasn't long before noblemen's sons began buzzing like bees around a flower before the table, each asking for a dance with her. She politely declined them all; she wanted to dance, desperately, but not with them. Sure, they were pretty to look at, but she usually preferred to dance alone or with a lady's maid, someone who wanted to take nothing from her, someone who wouldn't leech the fun from the flowing movements.

Her mother leaned over, bridging the gap between them for the second time that night, a slight flush to her bronze cheeks. "That last one was quite handsome. You should dance with him or another if he doesn't suit your fancy. Find someone to keep as a companion, you've earned it."

Xandrina raised her flute to her lips and took a tight-lipped sip, her shoulders stiffening at the implications her mother's tone seemed to stress on the word companion. She refused to make eye contact with her; she couldn't really be insinuating what Xandrina thought she was. "And if I don't wish to surround myself with companions?"

Her mother shrugged, a movement Xandrina felt in the brush of her mother's wing against hers more than she saw it. "That is your prerogative, dear, but I would remind you that it is tradition for an heir to keep at least a few noble sons, or daughters if you prefer; how close you allow them is up to you. Use them to run errands, rub your feet, or help you in the bath. It affords them status and appeases their families, many of which have sway with council members. You would do well to remember that now that you will have an active role in meetings as my heir."

Xandrina's lips curled. She knew that having her position solidified would come with complications, but what her mother suggested made her insides writhe like a wriggling mass of pond leeches. It was all so . . . unsavory. "So you want me to use them, to sway the council? That's reprehensible."

"It's not reprehensible, dear, it's politics. Never think for a second, they aren't trying to do the exact same thing. Each and every one of those families who've sent their sons to woo you is trying to maneuver you to their side one way or another, whether it's to earn them some more coin by swaying you to vote for more taxes on the commoners in their regions or to afford them more mining rights in the Pyramid Mountains. You just have to be clever enough to outmaneuver them and bend them to your will first."

Xandrina found herself nearly gaping at her mother. She snapped her mouth shut and lowered her eyes from her mother's fierce and stony face. It was well known the struggle her mother faced taking over after the Mad Queen passed on. She'd inherited a country rife with unrest with many council members outright opposed to having such a young queen on the throne. Many even went so far as to argue the dissolution of the throne entirely, an unprecedented power grab. Ultimately, she'd swayed them and took the throne that was rightfully hers. Xandrina had never asked what she'd done to change their minds, and by the time she was old enough to understand, her mother had long since set her aside. But had it truly been this? Had her mother been forced to let scummy and vile sons of councilmen attend her in her baths or let them touch her?

As if she could read her mind, her mother said, "You use whatever assets you have, daughter, no matter the cost, to protect our people, be it your blade, your brains, or your breasts, and you do it with pride knowing every sacrifice is for them."

Xandrina looked up again, meeting the full ferocity of her mother's molten gaze with her own. A silent understanding passed between them—unspoken words from mother to daughter, from queen to heir.

Chapter 5

The sphynx man who pulled her in time to the music across the dance floor was about as interesting as watching milk curdle. She couldn't remember his name, Ivan or Ivor or some such, and his blathering about his family estates by the sea was beginning to make her wish she could fling herself into the salty water he bragged incessantly about and drown herself just to be rid of him. He wasn't horrendous to look at, though, and he was less obnoxious than the one who'd come before him. Plus, seaside estates likely meant a relative with control over shipping lanes and trade routes, so she supposed he couldn't be outright dismissed.

If she thought of the men as pieces on a stones board, dancing with and manipulating them felt less abominable. Shuffle one here, nudge another there, and garner information and allies in court, it could be done. And who knew, maybe it could be fun, she was good at stones after all.

Cato and your mother say the Trials contestants are going to be presented soon. Finish your mating ritual with the pasty one and come back, Lyrahvi cooed from across the room where she sat coiled grooming herself in Xandrina's chair on the dais.

It's not a mating ritual, it's called dancing, Xandrina corrected through their bond, though she couldn't argue with calling him the pasty one. For someone who'd grown up by the sea on the edge of a desert, he had a surprisingly milky complexion and a slightly doughy physique that spoke of too many indulgences and long hours indoors. His spectacles made him look clever, though, and there was a witty twinkle in his turquoise eyes that she supposed could be construed as charming. Plus, he was tall, quite tall, which she discovered she rather liked in a dance partner.

He bowed to her as the song came to an end. His lips brushed across her hand, but only just barely as she breezed past him with a quick smile before he could ask her for another dance.

I think I'll watch from down here, get a closer look. She sent her giddy thoughts ahead to Lyrahvi who simply purred in response before Xandrina faded into the edge of the crowd at the base of the dais, just as a drum beat and trumpet heralded the spectacle to come.

Chapter 6

Ocidynus clapped a hand on Mutt's ridged shoulder as they assembled in formation with a jovial laugh. "Well, isn't this some shit, Mutt? Set your wing straight and quit gritting your teeth, boy. Smile, you want the sycophants to like you. You've got to work the crowd if you're to stand a chance at winning the Trial, that is."

"My fighting skills will speak for themselves in the Trial." The Mutt rolled his shoulders and made sure his sword belt was sitting straight for the tenth time to hide the slight tremor in his hands.

Oci swigged down the last of his wine, not the best he'd had, but it wasn't the normal army piss either, and set the cup on a table that seemed to serve no other purpose than to sit there and look pretty. "Your fighting will only get you so far. You want access to the best weapons in the Trial, maybe a concubine or two to suck your cock? Then when we get in there, you smile your ass off and flirt with some pretty nobles so they place their bets on you, and if their bets are on you, you better believe they'll do whatever they need to protect their investment."

The Mutt made a disgusted noise of disbelief in the back of his throat, but before he could argue, a horn blared, the thunder roll of drums sounded, and the doors of the banquet hall parted like the legs of an eager and well-paid whore. Which was essentially what all the gawking nobles were, whores for money and power. Maybe they didn't lie on their backs for it, but beneath all the sickeningly garish opulence that crusted their exterior, they were the same. Oci couldn't wait to bring them all to their knees.

Chapter 7

Abrax tried to listen attentively as the queen spoke of the honor and glory that came with winning the Trial and garnering one of the two most coveted positions in the kingdom for a fighting man, something they all knew, or they never would have signed up. But Abrax's focus kept slipping, his gaze drawn again and again back to the beautiful creature tucked at the base of the dais before them, wrapped in a spun gold dress and shimmering like a Fates-blessed ray of sun cutting through a thunderhead. She didn't gawk like the other milling nobles, their mouths gaping like dying fish, or point taloned fingers and titter, or ruffle her gorgeous wings excitedly. Instead, she appraised them all through coolly narrowed copper eyes as fastidious as a desert snake picking out its prey.

He'd been confident of winning one of the bonded guard positions since the sign-ups first started circulating through the barracks, but now a need like he'd never known before wrapped a fiery fist around his heart, stuttering its beats. If he won the position, maybe he could get to know her. It was a ridiculous notion, but when he looked at her, all he could hear were his mother's words whispering to him, death rattling at the edges of her voice, to be happy, to make a better life, to find love. Not that he was allowed to love, not like a normal sphynx, not as a bonded. No, bondeds were married to the position, but maybe he could love her from afar. An unrequited love, after all, was more love than he'd ever expected to get from this life.

Oci leaned in close, whispering gruffly at his ear so none could here, as the queen allowed them their leave to mingle and enjoy the celebration for the night. "Smile at that one, boy, and she's just as likely to bite your cock off as she is to suck it. Best find a safer one, perhaps that plump little one behind her there." Oci chuckled before stalking off through the crowd after a server with a tray full of chalices brimming with effervescently golden liquid that sparkled and bubbled under the moody light of the hanging globemallows.

After fighting with the older sphynx for most of his life, Abrax let his crassness roll off his back. The man was a brute but a kind one under it all. He glanced up at the dais, noting for the first time that the throne next to the queen's was empty; the princess hadn't even bothered to attend their presentation. What sort of self-absorbed female did she have to be to care so little about her potential bonding candidates? He shook his head, stuffing clenched fists into his pockets. Never mind that, he wanted to bond with the queen anyhow; it came with better pay and status. He turned his attention back to where the golden woman was only a heartbeat before, only to find her gone. He spun on the heel of his boot, scanning the milling and chattering crowd for her. He spotted her a moment later threading her way through the nobles and slipping her way out an open glass and rose-gold filagree door onto the less crowded balcony. Without too much thought, he followed as though she drew him to her by an invisible lead string.

The twinkling city lights blended into the starry sky above; potted plants perfumed the air with an intoxicating aroma. Abrax clung to the shadows cast by the palace wall just watching as the woman swayed her hips seductively, her head thrown back, in time with the music filtering through the open doors as she backed herself into a secluded corner with only the carved statue of a former queen he didn't know the name of for company.

He leaned against the stones of the palace wall, still warm from the day's heat, one foot kicked back against it, his arms crossed across his armored chest, and pretended to gaze out at the view of the capital while keeping one eye on her. She twirled, her skirts and her wings billowing ethereally around her, both catching the flickering light from the party within, making her radiant with coppery luminescence. Like a lucky coin on the street stones beckoning for a poor urchin boy to pluck it up and treasure it.

He stilled, his ribs constricting around his lungs as she slowed, and her near predatory gaze crashed into him like a fallen star crashing to the ground. She crooked a thin, delicate talon-tipped finger at him. "If you're going to stare at me like that, you could at least do me the courtesy of dancing with me first."

"Don't mind if I do, Princess." The rugged voice bloomed out of the darkness behind him. Abrax's hand jumped to the hilt of his dagger, silently cursing himself for getting so lost in a pretty face and sensuous body that he lost track of his surroundings. A bespectacled nobleman strode too confidently over to the—it struck him then—the noble had called her Princess. The word princess spelled itself around his heart and stilled its beating as his eyes flicked to her head where a thin golden circlet sat. He cursed himself for a fool for not having noticed, and of course, she'd not been speaking to him. Fates, how could he have thought even for a moment that she would demean herself by asking a lowly soldier like himself for a dance?

He took a step back, fading into the darkness from whence the nobleman had come, allowing the man who was far more deserving than he to gaze upon the princess's vicious and sharp beauty. And though he knew it was the right thing, he couldn't help but wonder at the weight that settled in his ribs at every step he took away from her.

Chapter 8

To Xandrina's dismay, the skulking soldier who'd been remarkably handsome, despite the burn scars that marred the side of his jaw and neck, bled into the shadows before disappearing entirely, rather than taking her hand and dancing with her. She'd been certain that he wanted to try and garner favor with her, maybe even petition her to sponsor him in the Trial. How utterly boring of him to scurry away into the night like a frightened child. Oh well, best she'd not gotten to know him, then. No one that meek would survive the Trial anyhow. Shame too, he'd been hard to make out swathed in darkness, but she'd caught a curious glimpse of his eyes, they were unlike anything she'd seen before, one as golden as the sun and the other as pale blue as the sky. It would be a shame to lose such a rarity to the Fate of Death.

She took the hand of the nobleman reluctantly, not wanting to be rude and dismiss him immediately, so she allowed him a few moments to dance with her in the shadows. His hands were all over her like a pair of wriggling serpents' tails. Clearly, he had some sort of ill-conceived notion that she'd intended something more by her invitation. She set him right swiftly, allowing her claws to elongate and press against his chest, not hard enough to make him bleed unfortunately, but hard enough that all the color slipped from his already pasty cheeks, and he coughed an abrupt excuse and all but ran from the balcony to no doubt spread gossip about her prickly nature.

As she watched the man disappear back inside, the statue behind her tapped her on the shoulder with a gray stone finger. She spun around to find Sarifella the Spiritual; she'd been one of Gypette's most pious queens, devoting her reign to building the spires that dotted the cityscape in the name of the Fates so that the people could pray to them. Some legends about her even claimed she could speak to the Fates themselves. This was the first time she'd ever deigned to speak to Xandrina, though, and come to think of it, it might have been the first time she'd spoken to any queen that the princess knew of. The long-dead queen's fingers twisted to sign the words, "Congratulations, heir, on winning your crown."

Xandrina made her own fingers twist in response, warmth spreading like hot caramel to candy coat her heart, *Heir*, the title was hers at last. "Thank you, Majesty."

"Be wary and wise, hold your wits and your heart in a vise. The Fates look on, but even they are afraid of what is to come."

Fear ran its icy claws down her back, setting her feathers on edge. She grasped Sarifella's carved hands before she could slip away, the weathered stone chafing against her palms. "What is so terrible that the Fates fear it? What is coming?"

The queen's statue pulled away and shook its head morosely as she signed. "I cannot say, Heir, but heed my warning and beware, they will not interfere."

Chapter 9

Oci disentangled himself from the concubines draped sleepily over him. Fates be damned but those women were good at their job. He hadn't slept that well since, well fuck, he couldn't remember when. He ducked out into the hall and strode naked down to the communal bathing chamber in the building that housed the Trial combatants. The accommodation was better than any army outpost he'd be stationed at. Each combatant had their own room and their pick of women and wine. It was the least the crown could do since they might lose their lives, or if they were lucky, just a limb or two in the fight to come.

He dove into the steaming bath, stirring the pink mist that snaked along the surface, some sort of exotic healing waters piped in from hot springs in the desert beyond the oasis, or something like that. One of the concubines had explained it last night while trying to make small talk before he'd given her mouth something better to do.

Rolling his shoulders, he stretched his wings out, letting the thin skin soak in the luxurious warmth with a sigh. Never had he imagined comfort such as this in all his years a slave and a soldier. But this was just the beginning. There was a long way yet to go to make what was whispered to him in those darkest depths come true.

The Mutt skulked in, dark circles smudged under his peculiar eyes. His hair was shorn on the sides, the rest, usually knotted on the top, hung loose and disheveled. "What's the matter with you, Mutt? Did you smile at that golden girl last night? I told you that one was liable to bite your . . ."

"I'm fine, Oci, give it a rest already," Abrax snipped as he splashed inelegantly into the large pool, dunking his head under the water before resurfacing, sputtering, and wiping a hand down his stubbled face.

"Sorry, kid, rough night?" Oci knew better than anyone what Abrax had been through. The kid hadn't been in the mines, not like he had, he was too young for that, but as a half breed, he hadn't had it easy either. They'd fought together in the Isles during a handful of skirmishes against harpie raiders in battles where the blood flowed so freely the sea was crimson as far as the eye could see. He'd barely lived through that one. A harpie bitch had gotten her clawed feet wrapped around his throat; he still had the small talon point scars on his neck to remember her by. Abrax had been the one to cut the bitch down, ran her through with his sword. If Oci thought on it too long, he could still taste the tang of her blood as it spilled hot across his face as if he were being anointed by the Fate of War.

Abrax shrugged, laying his head back against the tiled rim of the tub as other sphynx groggily filtered in stinking of stale alcohol and sex. "No better or worse than any other night I suppose," he deflected.

"Nightmares again?" It was a rhetorical question—every soldier, especially the ones here, knew that once the nightmares started, they didn't ever stop. Mutt didn't answer, but his silence was all the confirmation he needed. Oci stood from the bath, letting the water drip off his skin a moment before grabbing a towel to wrap around his waist. "You get your head on straight before we head into that arena today, kid, or you're going to be meat for the beasts come sundown."

"I'm good. I've got it handled," the Mutt muttered with enough steel on the edges of his words that Oci nearly believed him.

Oci almost argued with him, he wanted to grab the kid by his hair and shake the fight back into him, but a hiss that echoed like claws against his mind from a distance stilled his tongue. From this moment on, Mutt was his competition in the Trial ahead, and he could let nothing stand in his way.

Chapter 10

Safiya lounged next to her daughter in the royal box above the arena, watching the opening ceremonies of the Trial. She tried to spot the man she'd noted the night before, the valkry with the astonishingly golden eyes, arrogant smirk, and infectious laugh that she could hear from across the ballroom. He was such a curiosity, she'd seen valkry before, of course, when her mother dragged her on her victory progress to visit the smoldering ruins of their once great nation. The valkry she'd seen then had been broken, beaten, a people so downtrodden they were sure to never rise again. Conquering their nation was to be her mother's legacy. Safiya thumbed the scar across her lips as the memory of the whip crack that caused it flashed across her thoughts like lightning striking the desert sands as it often did when she remembered her mother. She quelled the sickening memories and turned her gaze back on the arena. She didn't relish the thought of watching the brutality that was to come unfold. Despite being raised a warrior as all the queens of her line had been, Safiya abhorred violence. She had seen enough of it to paint her nightmares in blood for the rest of her days.

Next to her, her daughter cheered with the rest of the onlookers, though with slightly more poise, as befitted her station, she clapped and stomped feet, but she did not rise from the edge of her seat.

"Did you meet any last night worth keeping your eye on?" Safiya asked as a flash of leathery black wings drew her eyes to the fray of men and beasts battling below. The sight of him stole her breath from her lungs. She imagined it drifting down to where he fought, the corded muscles of his arms on full display, to tuck itself beneath his black breastplate by his heart like a prayer to the Fate of Luck.

Xandrina shifted slightly, it was a simple stiffening that most would overlook, but Safiya saw it for what it was, her daughter bracing herself for a lie. It was a tell she'd had since her very first fib when she'd snuck her little fingers into her birthday cake frosting before it was time to cut. "I can't say that I did," she replied, her words as tight as her posture.

It stung, like nettles wrapped around her heart, that her daughter would lie to her, but she also couldn't blame her. They'd spoken more times in the past few days than they had in years. Trust was a bridge built brick by brick over time in need of constant upkeep and maintenance, and theirs had been left to decay.

"You'll have to learn to lie better than that, my heir." Safiya meant the words in jest, mostly, because learning to spin the truth was essential to running the country, but Xandrina just nodded curtly.

"As you say, Mother." Those nettles dug into Safiya's heart harder, squeezing like a fist, until pain wept from the wounds. She had no one to fault but herself for letting her daughter in in the first place, for pushing her away. She could try to lay the blame on the assassins sent in the dark so long ago, on her own mother for only taking an interest in her when she was nearing the age of readiness for her ordeal so she had no good example of what a mother's love should be. But to place blame at another's feet would do her no good, and it would repair nothing between them now. Not when it was likely too late.

Beside her Xandrina sighed, her shoulders relaxed but only just a hair as she leaned forward to stroke the top of her Tatzelwurm's head where it lay curled at her feet. "There was one soldier, with strange eyes. I admit I was curious about him, but he ended up being nothing but a disappointment."

Another lie, but Safiya's lips curled into a slight smile as she realized this lie was not meant for her but was one her daughter seemed to be telling herself. Maybe there was a sliver of hope that the bridge could be rebuilt after all.

Chapter 11

To Oci, the smell of battle was always the same no matter whose blood was on your sword. It smelled of the coppery tang of blood, of course, tasted of it too, but what the ballads failed to mention was the stench of piss and shit and burning flesh.

Not that he noticed when the icy calm settled over him. No, the realization, the smells, the sounds always came to him once the sword fell in a startling crash one atop the other like boulders in a rockslide. It weighed on his heart and in his dreams as it did with every battle-worn being.

In the moment, though, all he knew was the dance. The patterns of jabs, thrusts, and swinging arcs that landed blows that both maimed and murdered the beasts and other contestants around him. The Trial presented them all with a writhing mass of fears, much as he'd heard it did with the princess the day before. But instead of their own, it was the fears of the royals whom they were hoping to win the right to guard. That suited him fine, he could handle the fears of others, it was the terrors of his own mind that he did not wish to face, that he didn't wish to have conjured for all to see.

So in his calm void, he hacked and slashed and stayed alive because he had to live, and more importantly, he had to win.

Chapter 12

Xandrina's eyes caught on the spot where Abrax's blood dripped to the floor of the royal arena box, mixing with his sweat filling the vicinity with the smells of copper and salt so strong she could taste it in the back of her throat. She coolly arched a brow, keeping her face impassive even as a strange mixture of excitement and apprehension sluiced through her veins at the sight of him standing there battered and bruised. "Oh, it's you, the lurker. I must say, I didn't think you had it in you." And of all things he'd chosen her. As first victor on the field, slaying the most beasts and impressively subduing the valkry, the second victor, with efficient, cold precision. He'd earned the right to choose whom to bond first, and instead of taking the glory that was rightfully his, bonding the queen—her stomach free-fell at the thought, even as she kept her face smooth and unreadable—he'd chosen her.

Ire, or something very nearly like it, flashed swiftly through his strange eyes so quickly if she'd blinked, she would not have caught it. Oh, he did not like to be underestimated. *He's meaty this one,* Lyrahvi hissed from her perch on Xandrina's shoulder, *like a snack. If you don't eat him, I will.* Xandrina took a sip of the sweetly spiced wine from her chalice to hide her smile, meaty indeed.

"If I'm not up to your standards, my lady, then perhaps you could hold the Trial again and find someone more to your liking. Though I can assure you, I'd win them again." The words were delivered with gentlemanly grace but also with a bite of sarcasm, surprising for an army brute. The message underneath was clear as well: *I can play your games, Princess.*

Her lips twisted into a venomous smile, and she waved a dismissive hand in his direction. "No, I suppose you'll have to do. Go get yourself cleaned up and healed, you're getting blood all over the floor."

"As you wish, Your Highness." He bowed, but his smoldering eyes darted one last hooded glance her way before he turned his back to her and strode out of the box, slamming the door in his wake.

Puuurrrr, snack is going to be good fun.

Xandrina wholeheartedly agreed.

Chapter 13

Safiya rubbed the frustration from between her brows as she tried to listen to the bickering council members shout at one another across the table. She must have angered the Fates somehow, for never in the history of Gypette had there been a dispute over a bonded's appointment, Of course, there had never been a valkry who won, let alone enter the competition. The poor man had earned his place fair and square. If it had been anyone else, she would be preparing for the bonding ceremony now instead of listening to this dribble. Of course, there was one small blessing in that they had yet to comment on her daughter's bonded who also had valkry blood, though only by half, so maybe she hadn't lost *all* Fates' favor.

She pressed two fingers to her temple, idly massaging as she leaned on her armrest and let the council have their fit, not unlike letting a babe run through their tantrum before they settled enough to listen to rationality. "He's going to be the ruin of this kingdom; Fates mark my words." Fayden brandished a gnarled finger to make his point. "Their kind have been a scourge upon this land, a blight -"

"Enough." Safiya rolled her eyes and stood, bracing her hands on the table. She was tired of her mother's beliefs haunting her reign. "That's old rhetoric from a time long past, Councilman, and I don't care for it in my chambers. If you can't get that through your head, then perhaps it is time for you to step down and let someone with a sharper wit take your seat at this table."

The insufferable man had just enough good sense to stop talking, though he ruffled his gray feathers indignantly and his jowls worked as he chewed on his unsaid words. Fine by her, he could choke on them for all she cared.

"Now as for the valkry." She looked at each member of her council in turn, making sure they felt the full weight and sincerity of her next words, the full weight of the throne. "He won the Trial, one of our most sacred and ancient rituals, and he will become my bonded as is decreed by our laws, and I will hear no more slander in regard to his heritage. Furthermore, I'm glad he won; his appointment to this prestigious role is an integral step toward healing a nation that has never stepped off the precipice of the senseless war started by my mother."

"Your mother did what was necessary -" Fayden started to rise as though possessed by the ghost of her mother's reign.

"I will hear no more, Fayden. Fates mark my words," she hissed through clenched teeth, "this is the last time my mother is mentioned around this council table, or it will not only be your seat I take from you, but your properties as well. Just because I'm not my mother does not mean I won't do whatever I feel is necessary to uphold the laws of our country. Council is adjourned." She stiffened her spine and stalked from the room to the sound of victorious silence from those she left behind, across the mosaicked floor, and out into the hallway where the valkry stood waiting.

She thumbed her scar and looked him over from his face covered in drying ichor to his wings scarred with the marks of battles past. He stood at ease, his hand on the hilt of his sword, his golden eyes plainly searching her as much as she searched him, though what he hoped to see was unclear. "I'll see you at the bonding, valkry, the title of Queen's bonded is yours."

Chapter 14

Guilt and sorrow still filled Safiya like sand whenever she thought of her first bonded guard. She'd been far too young, not even named heir yet, but so was he. Victrus was honorable and kind. He'd always snuck her favorite honey cakes from the kitchens when the Mad Queen was in one of her moods and restricted her food. They both loved the same books, he was an exceptional stones player, and he would sing dirty bar ballads to cheer her up. Her mother had plucked him on a paranoid whim from his happy life and had him tied to her daughter without trial, at the point of her knife. But together they had made the best of it.

If Safiya had known then that bonding her would be the death of him, she would have fought against it harder. He was buried without honor in the desert, branded a traitor to the crown for defending her against her mother, but she knew where his grave was and visited every so often to sing the songs of mourning.

She tried to shove memories of him aside, tucking him back in his tomb to find that peaceful rest that only the dead could have, as her handmaid, Marryn, swept her hair into a half coronet of braids and a waterfall of curls. She chatted away behind her, talking of this and that, feeding her bits of useful gossip that she'd picked up throughout her day. Safiya dipped her fingers into the clay pot of perfumed hand cream and massaged it into her claw beds and up her forearms as she met the woman's gaze in the mirror. "The valkry, Marryn, what morsels of information have you scavenged where he is concerned?"

Marryn flushed a pretty shade of pink. "Well I, well, he's quite the philanderer, my Queen, though a generous one if the courtesan's gossip is to be believed."

"Have any in my employ tended to his needs?" She'd spent many a year cultivating a group of loyal women, the unseen ones, the ones that could pass through any circle of life undetected—florists, whores, midwives, barmaids, cooks—her eyes and ears in a world of men who would rather keep her blind.

Marryn tapped her plump chin thoughtfully. "No, but Sylvanna might be able to get to him, she seems his type, shall I send her tonight?" Sylvanna was a slip of a woman, sinuous and beautiful with pale golden hair and bright eyes. She was fiercely loyal to Safiya who'd found her in the Pit's gutter, cast aside and beaten by a patron. Safiya brought her to the palace, tendered to her visible wounds, and offered her a job where she'd never have to lie on her back for any man again if she didn't want to. She still often chose to as a means of extracting information, but everything was always within her control.

"No, that won't be necessary." Something ugly reared its head from deep within her viscera, at the thought of her guard bedding a woman on the night of their bonding, but she didn't want to look at the feeling too closely. "Is there anything else I should know?" She'd vouched for this man to the council, so she needed to know that her instincts about him weren't wrong, that he wasn't harboring an ill intent toward her or her kingdom despite the tragedy done to his people in the past.

Her maid placed two Sea of Callais pearls in each of her lobes before pulling her crown from its velvet-lined box on the vanity and setting it atop her head. "No, Majesty, but I'll let you know at once if I hear even the faintest of whispers."

Safia stood smoothing her hands over her skirts. "Thank you. And please"—she set a hand on Marryn's shoulder—"take the rest of the night and tomorrow off. Go join the festivities."

Marryn beamed and curtsied before she rushed from the room singing her gratitude over her shoulder. Safiya paused, taking one last look at herself in the vanity mirror, before she too slipped out into the hall to go meet the man with whom she was to tie not only her soul, but also her fate.

Chapter 15

Xandrina was dressed in the softest linen sheath, the color of billowing vermilion clouds at sunset, her waist accentuated with a wrapped, braided golden cord. Her circlet, expertly twined into hair that was half up and half down by the deft hands of her maid, matched the golden bangles at her wrists and ankles.

The secluded garden she waited in hummed with life buzzing along the intoxicating perfumed breeze that teased her feathers and lifted the ends of her hair to the fading sun making sure it illuminated each coppery strand. The bonding ceremony was ritually a private one, with only the pair to be bound in attendance. There were no formal words or incantations to be spoken, though vows were often freely given. Xandrina was quite unsure what she would say when the man finally appeared. Her thoughts were all tangled in knots, as was her stomach, as she paced the small shrubbed alcove that overlooked the distant oasis, expanding and retracting her claws with the flick of her fingers as she did.

She'd wanted to ask her mother what to expect, beyond the procedure for sealing the bond, which was a simple swapping of blood through a slice across the palms. No, she wanted to know what it was like to have someone's life so entwined with your own, but it was a sensitive subject for the queen, so Xandrina had bitten her tongue. She regretted that now. *Stop your fidgeting. You will make Snack nervous when he comes.* Lyrahvi's voice came as a whisper.

I'm not fidgeting, merely thinking, she thought back at the Tatzelwurm acerbically. *Besides, you can't possibly know what I'm doing when you're not here to see.*

I don't need to be there to see you when I can FEEL you, Princess. Her voice curled around Xandrina's mind with lilted laughter. *You're more nervous than a Gorgishan foal on shearing day.*

Annoyance curled Xandrina's lip, but she steeled herself, stiffening her spine, and turned to brace her hands against the railing that overlooked the vast Kedlaya Oasis. Its waters were the perfect mirror image of the sunset so that you could almost imagine that the boats that drifted lazily on the rippling water were sailing through the melted sherbet sky instead. She took a deep breath in and held it, counting slowly until it felt as though her ribs would crack, and only then did she relinquish her hold on it. She was a princess, and the heir, she'd faced monsters both real and conjured, surely, she could bond with one man and come out of it unchanged.

"Highness." The soldier's voice bloomed, husky and sweet behind her. She glanced over her shoulder at him. He cleaned up rather nicely, his broad shoulders filling his black tunic under his leather armor, his hair knotted back, still slightly damp from his bath.

She frowned at him and at the twinge of nerves that flogged her heart and sent it thrashing in her chest. "You're late."

"I'm not. The bell won't sound for another few moments at least." He stepped into the alcove to stand opposite her. The small space seemed to shrink in on itself, as though the very air around them drew closer to get a better view, and Xandrina was struck with the sudden understanding for why such a moment as this was done in private.

She reached into the slit of her sheath that ran the length of her leg all the way to her thigh and produced her dagger with a flourish that lit up the soldier's eyes, though with what she couldn't say. "Well, let's get on with it, then." She gestured impatiently toward his hands.

He held out his palm obediently, like an offering on a Fate's altar. She took it, acutely aware of how hot it felt against hers, how scarred and calloused his caramel skin already was, and in the briefest moment of hesitation, as she brought the silver tip of her dagger to his flesh, she wondered what sort of life he'd had that led him here to this moment. In a quick slash, she split the skin across his palm and watched it peel apart like a ripped seam. His crimson blood began to well in earnest.

Deftly and without asking, he took the dagger from her and encircled her wrist, drawing her nondominant hand close. Her blood crashed through her veins, pounding through her ears louder than a war drum, as he swiftly drew the knife tip across her palm and pressed his bloodied hand into hers.

She stared at the place where their hands met, the tangled metallic scent of their mingled blood flooded the small space, overrunning the smell of the night-blooming flowers that unfurled their sleepy heads and rubbed blinking eyes to gaze upon the pair of them. The combined wounds throbbed with such force that it felt as though they pressed hearts together rather than palms.

Abrax hooked two fingers from his free hand under her chin and tilted her face until she met the intensity of his gaze. "I, Abrax, hereby vow by the Fates to be your bonded protector from this moment forward. I will come when you call and guard your heart as though it were my own. From this day until the Fate of Death steals my last breath, I will always be at your back through blood and ruin."

The princess stared, raw unfiltered awe coursing through her. This man before her meant what he said with his whole being, she could feel it, could feel him, inside her. It was not like the starkly clear words she could hear from Lyrahvi, but she could sense his sincerity, his every emotion as though it were part of her and yet . . . not. Like she'd just allowed him to stitch a part of himself onto her soul.

"Do you . . ." She blinked, drawing herself back into her own head, the part of her that remained untouched by the bond, the part of her that was who she was at her core, and that part teemed with inexplicable emotions, irritation, frustration, embarrassment, in a pit-like spiraling mass. She wished she had words as eloquent as his, she was, after all, a learned woman, so she should be able to form a coherent vow, but instead, the words that tumbled from her parted lips tripped over one another in an embarrassing snag. "Yes, well, bond and guard each other's backs, yes, all of that, good, thank you."

She yanked her hand back, immediately and instinctively drew on her magic, a thread of deep cosmic beauty to suture her wound shut. Without even considering what it meant, she did the same for Abrax, sending a thread to bridge the gap between them.

He stared down at his palm, curiosity and something like astonishment scrawled across his strange eyes as she backed out of the alcove. She needed space, distance would surely put a damper on the sensations that pulsed from that tangled bit of him, but a moment later, his footsteps were behind her, an echo to her own. She cast a furious glance over her shoulder. "You don't have to hound me, you know. I'm perfectly safe here in my home."

He shrugged. "It's my duty, Highness, to protect you at all times."

She huffed a sigh so wrapped in exasperation it was nearly venomous and continued walking toward her rooms. How in the Fates was she supposed to live with a man's emotions knotted up next to her own? And how in the fuck was he remaining so placidly calm about this? Surely, he had to feel her as well; the bond was two sided like a coin. No man was that unflappable.

Oh, my poor pet, who knew bonding Snack would get you so riled up, Lyrahvi crooned a laugh.

It's not funny, Lyra, I can't focus with him in my head! She hated the sharp-edged panic that tinted the edges of her words as she stormed down that marble-tiled hall, her neck ached from resisting the urge to cast glances over her shoulder at her guard.

Then bury it like a bad dream, deep in your mind where you won't feel it. If left open, you'll be able to sense his emotions and eventually his thoughts. Those who are bonded for a lifetime can even feel one another's pain, but if you close it off and hide it, you will feel none of that. Her hiss was almost bored, riddled with condescension as though the concept were something a babe should know.

It's really just as simple as that? Xandrina poked the edges of cool, stony, emotions nestled in her head disbelievingly.

Would I lie to you? She severed their connection, slamming the mental door insultedly, between their minds.

Xandrina paused in the hallway, and the steps behind her blessedly stilled. She closed her eyes, tipped her head back, and relaxed her wings. She could visualize him there like a dark moon nestled in the nebulousness of her mind. She gave it a gentle shove to no avail, then a firmer shove, throwing the weight of her magic behind it. It waned, slowly, fading from full and brilliant, radiating feeling, to the shadow of a new moon, there but not directly noticeable unless you knew where to look for it.

She let out a sigh strangled with relief and leaned against the mental door between her and Lyra. She whispered her thanks, to which she thought she heard an indistinct grumbled response.

Fates be blessed, she was free of him. She cast a copper-eyed glance behind her where Abrax waited patiently—well, not free of him exactly, but at least she had her wits back.

Chapter 16

The Feast of Fifty Days began with the tolling of bells. Abrax watched Princess Xandrina, a slow and lazy smile curled along her lips as she lay draped and a little intoxicated along her balcony railing, her skirts and wings dangling on either side like a rug taken out for beating.

The city below them lay dark, and then as the first bell tolled out, a lonely cry in the night, a solitary light blossomed in the dark followed by another and another and another as citizens below lit lanterns, each new luminescent light birthed with a chime. Then in a billowing cloud of light, they released them all simultaneously into the night air to dance to a symphony of bells.

The princess laughed giddily, the sound of it somehow seeming to loop around his heart and pull.

The Tatzelwurm wouldn't take her eyes off him, occasionally licking her lips and brandishing her fangs in what might have been a smile. He had yet to work up the nerve to ask Xandrina if it was going to slip into his adjoining bedchamber and eat him while he slept. She seemed like the sort that would keep a deadly pet, just for the thrill of it.

For a few blissful moments, he'd been able to feel her in his head as clearly as if her emotions were his own, and it was radiant. But then she'd severed the connection somehow or dulled it, swaddling it in secrecy. Not that he supposed he could blame her, she didn't know him, and he didn't know her, but he wanted to, more desperately and urgently than he'd ever wanted to know anyone before.

"Bonded." Xandrina giggled from where she slid off the railing, fortunately on the right side of it. He didn't want to have to perform any daring rescue-flight maneuvers just now; he was a skilled flier, but it was more difficult in the dark and when the person you were trying to save was so wildly inebriated. "Isn't it pretty, don't they look like stars?" She hiccuped inelegantly, and Fates if it wasn't adorable. He tried not to laugh as he looked up at the illuminated orbs drifting aimlessly against a crushed-velvet sky.

"They do," he agreed softly. When he looked back down, her head had lolled to the side, and her eyelashes kissed her cheeks.

Stop staring at her, Snack, and put her to bed. Abrax's pupils flared as he looked in awe at the Tatzelwurm. It raised itself up and perched on the end of its tail so that its more catlike portions were looking at him directly though, not quite in the eye, he still towered over it, and the princess for that matter.

Did you just call me a snack? He cocked his head, a skeptical eyebrow raised.

The Tatzelwurm sighed. *I have many things I can call you, Snack is just my favorite, but I have several nastier names if you don't do as you're told and put her to bed before the chill of the night sets in. She can't sleep here.*

You can talk? he asked, suspicion and disbelief warring on his face.

Come now, Snack, prove to me you're not all meat and that you have some brains between your ears. You are bonded to Pet; I can talk to her, and so now I can talk to you. The creature crossed its arms and rolled its eyes at him.

He chuckled and knelt to get a better look at her. *I'm not sure whether I should be honored you're talking to me or concerned you call me Snack.*

You'll be dead if you don't do as I say and get the heir to the throne inside. But she preened a little at his flattery as she said it.

Abrax nodded his head in silent acquiescence and stood, scooping Xandrina into his arms as he did so. He ignored how she felt curled against his chest and the strange things it did to his heart. He crossed the threshold into her chamber, her wings trailing on the floor as they walked, and settled her on her bed. He drew a blanket up over her, and the corner of his mouth tipped in a smile as she muttered incoherently in her sleep. She looked so peaceful, and Fates damned beautiful when she slept; all the entitlement and venom leeched out of her.

The Tatzelwurm crawled up onto the bed and curled next to the princess, her head resting protectively on the swell of her hip. *Go to bed, Snack. I'll watch her from here.*

He looked around the room for an excuse to stay, which seemed silly. The room was clear, the hall doors were locked, and the wurm could call him if anything seemed amiss, but there was a fluttery, unnamable feeling in his gut that he should not leave. That something was off.

Dismissing it as just a settling of nerves after an eventful few days, he nodded once to the wurm and slipped through the adjoining door to his small suite and let the door fall shut with a soft click of the latch.

The space was not ornate by the rest of the palace's standards he was sure, but to him it was pure luxury. His bed was full, with a real mattress, more than one blanket, and enough space for his wings to stretch out. He had a small bathing room all to himself and a closet to store his meager belongings, his army trunk already tucked inside by an attentive staff. But best of all, he had a window, slight though it may be, that let in a shaft of ivory incandescent moonlight to slant across the tiled floor.

Abrax made quick work of his buckles and armor, years of practice taking it off and putting it on again in a hurry had trained his muscles to do it without much thought, and tucked them away on the hooks in his closet. He sat on the bed, its cords drawn so tight beneath the frame that it didn't even groan, and undid his boots and britches. He tucked the former just under the bed as he always had and the latter he hung over the end of the bed frame should he need to find them quickly in the dark. He stripped off his tunic and laid it with his pants.

He climbed into bed and settled under the covers. Before he let sleep claim him, he palmed the small wooden carving that hung on a leather cord around his neck and ran a finger over the planes of the face he'd whittled from memory. "I did as I promised, Mother," he whispered to her likeness. "I made a better life. I just wish you were here to see it."

Chapter 17

The sense of Ocidynus's emotions in Safiya's head were muted almost the instant the bond locked into place save for a tiny dark sliver that pricked when plucked out, one with a sharpness that made her leery until she shoved it away without examining it closer. Whether she did the masking unconsciously or he had prior knowledge of how to block, she didn't know, but either way she was grateful for it. She'd felt one bonded die already, and that was more than enough pain. It had very nearly killed her. If she hadn't been able to channel that rage into destroying her mother and taking the throne, it would have eviscerated her. She would have to remember to tell Xandri how to do it next time they crossed paths and silently scolded herself for not remembering to tell her before.

She drew a tendril of her power through her itching fingers and soothed it over the edges of the slash across her palm. Her magic, like her daughter's, looked like the cosmos, though where Xandrina's had always been dark and nebulous, hers was golden and studded with stars. Her bonded frowned down at her glowing fingers. "Here, let me, I can heal yours too. Admittedly, I'm not as good with healing as I should be, but it will take the pain and speed along the process."

To her surprise, he pulled his hand back, almost petulantly, yanked out a strip of bandage from his pocket and, wadded it around his palm with a shake of his head. "I'm fine," he ground out. "I've had worse."

Safiya sighed; he would have to be a stubborn one wouldn't he. She shrugged. "Have it your way. I just didn't want to let any would-be assassins get the advantage over you and kill me because you can't hold your sword properly."

He grunted, practically rolling his eyes, but he didn't acquiesce. Stupid. Stubborn. Males.

Safiya pulled her dark-navy cloak, the exact shade of the midnight sky above them, over her shoulders, allowing her wings to slip through the holes in the back, and pulled up the cowl over her loose auburn curls before she turned and walked toward the courtyard that led to a discreet side gate.

"Where are you going?" Oci growled, still rooted to the spot in the gardens where they'd exchanged bond vows. His golden eyes flashed in the moonlight.

"I guess you'll have to follow me and find out," she teased over her shoulder. Really, did he expect guarding her would mean just standing next to her while she sat like a doll on the throne?

His heavy-booted feet stomped after her a moment later, and she thought she caught grumbling under his breath that sounded like string of curses and comments regarding flighty and evasive women.

Safiya sighed, a small smile tugged at the edges of her scarred lips. The brute was going to take some polishing.

Chapter 18

Oci kept a cold fist wrapped around their bond in a tight grip as he stalked irritably behind the queen down the lively halls packed with revelers celebrating the heir and the Trail. A few minutes of being bonded to her and she was already different than he'd expected, not that he'd set his expectations high. He'd pictured someone pampered who would lounge about in gardens with servants to feed her sweets. She did, after all, have a reputation as being a soft-handed queen, especially when compared to the blood-thirsty reign of her mother. She didn't conquer, simply defended against harpie raids. She freed slaves rather than chain them and haul them away to the darkest depths of the mines. Oci ground his teeth; he didn't want to think about the differences between her and the bloodhungry bitch that took everything from him. He couldn't afford to see the queen as anything other than the crown and what the crown had done to him and his people.

The queen cut down a shadowy hall and through a door that let out into a circular open space, hemmed in by flowering shrubs. At its heart was one of the famed spires sprouted from a patch of grass threaded through with narrow irrigation channels, quaint pathways, and foot bridges. Its tip speared the sky as though it hoped to pierce the heart of the moon and watch it bleed silver across the sky.

Oci dogged the queen's steps as she approached the narrow tower; she paused on the threshold and turned to face him. "You can wait here, bonded. I doubt there is an assassin lurking in this place of worship."

He couldn't help but smile at the irony. An assassin was, after all, what he technically was, though he wasn't just after her life. "I think not, Your Majesty."

She rolled her eyes but tucked her wings, hiked her skirts, and proceeded into the spindly building anyhow without further argument. Oci had never been one for prayers, not when the Fates so clearly wanted to fuck him. It was far narrower than he'd expected, nothing but stone walls and stairs that went round and round and round dizzyingly. He tried to force his gaze straight ahead on the queen's back to steady the whirling sensation, but that proved to be an even bigger mistake as her amply round ass was in his direct line of sight, and what an unfortunately nice ass it was. His blood rushed from his head, and he cleared his throat. "I think I'll wait here, give you some privacy in your, eh, worship."

A small smirk twisted her scarred lips as she looked at him over her shoulder. "As you wish, bonded." And then in a rush of skirts, she was gone, leaving Oci to twist his broad frame around agonizingly in the slight space until he was leaning sort of comfortably against the wall, ready to descend when she finished. Fates be fucked, he hoped she didn't take too long.

He was just about to get irritable when a song like a memory drifted down, echoing around the bends of the stone wall to caress his thoughts, pulling up the haunting image of a face hovering above him, eyes shining and filled with kindness and love. It was a face he'd buried long ago, for when it came to him, it was usually twisted with fear and spattered with blood. Was that the power of prayer that he'd been missing? The ability to see the face of your long-dead mother in the notes of another's song? Something in the vision of her soft features made the stone around his heart fracture like the seedling of a mighty tree trapped in the crevasse of a mountain sending out its first roots.

The song ended, but the vision remained. He tucked it away gently, afraid if he set it aside too forcefully it would break, and he would once again only be able to see the nightmarish opposite. Oci felt the queen's presence on the stairs without having to turn around and look, not in his bond, but in the way the hairs rose on the back of his neck.

In that precise moment, it dawned on him that he may have gotten himself in far too deep.

Chapter 19

Safiya let the last notes of her sung prayers scatter along on the night air like the fluffy white fragments of a flower gone to seed blown by children making wishes. She stood and surveyed the view of her kingdom from the precipice, her heart full, and she felt for the first time in her life that perhaps all the prayers she'd sung and whispered for so long were coming true. Her nation was healing, albeit slowly, from the horrors of her mother's reign, her valkry bonded was proof of that, and her daughter was heir. She allowed herself a small, satisfied smile. Maybe, just maybe it was time to pull out those other dreams, for her and for her kingdom, the ones that she'd once thought were too far flung and hopeful, and give them another look.

She turned to go, but a movement in the recessed shadows caught her eye. "Who goes there?" she said in hushed tones, not wanting to speak too loudly and summon her guard. Her heart drifted into her throat as a cloud passed over the moon, deepening the shawl of darkness wrapped around the lurker. "Name yourself." She threaded the words with a magical command.

The silhouetted form stepped closer, and Safiya took a step back, the carved balcony balustrade biting into her backside as she summoned a lick of gilded celestial flame to her palm. She held it up and sighed. "Ah, it is just you."

The statue of the dead queen Sarifella the Spiritual slid forward. She often hid at the top of the spire, her soul still in communion with the Fates, or so Safiya assumed. The marble woman never communicated beyond flinty glances or a nod of her head. Safiya bobbed a slight curtsy to her ancestor, little more than a dip and a flutter of her skirt. She always felt like she was on her back foot with the deceased queens who haunted the palace, never knowing quite how to act. "I shall leave you to your prayer," she murmured, but before she could take more than a step, Sarifella barred her way, wedging herself between Safiya and the narrow door.

Sarifella raised her fingers and began to speak. *To your death you must go hasty and willing to save your heir's blood from spilling.*

The sweetly perfumed air suddenly felt noxious, each breath choked, nauseatingly thick in Safiya's lungs. She raised her hands to reply to ask . . . to ask what, she did not know. There were too many questions wriggling and stirring, clamoring in her mind and jumbling together. To her death, was it now, this moment? To save her heir, what danger was her daughter in? Who would spill her blood?

The statue surprised her by running a cool hand across her cheek in a soothing motion. *You should not evade this end, unfortunate though it may be. To death's will, you must bend, for if you resist, both you and your heir will perish. Upon you our line depends, nod if you understand.*

She did not understand, but numbly, she nodded anyhow.

The deceased queen began to move away, but it was Safiya's turn to bar her path, dancing her fingers as swiftly as she could. "It is certain that if I die willingly, my daughter will live? The Fates have said so? Is it promised?"

Sarifella looked at the stars and then back at Safiya. If she saw the expression etched on any other's face, Safiya would have called it sorrowful. *There are things the Fates cannot see, but your willing sacrifice should pay the required price.*

"But who?" Safiya pleaded, but Sarifella shook her head.

No more can be said. And then she wrapped herself again in the shadows, her carved face upturned in prayer, leaving Safiya to smooth her features and return below as though her heart and her hopes had not just been shattered.

Chapter 20

Xandrina crept on tiptoes across the floor of her room and into her dressing room. She quickly shed her formal dress and unraveled her hair, gently setting her circlet on her vanity before rummaging in the back behind her most voluminous ball gowns to find the loose board in the floor. She unfurled a single long claw, slipped it beneath the floorboard, and jiggled until it popped open with a dusty groan. Inside was a bundle of neatly folded merchant-class clothes bought discreetly in a shop on her most recent unsanctioned trip into the city.

There was no way she was going to miss the first of the Fifty Feasts; she could hear music on the wind, and her feet yearned to dance where none knew her or wanted to manipulate her. Abrax had been surprisingly easy to trick; he never suspected that she was playing at being intoxicated, drinking sparking juice instead of wine. He'd been surprisingly tender tucking her into bed, to the point she almost felt guilty about lying to him. Almost. But there was no way that straitlaced soldier would understand the ache in her soul to be among her people as nothing but one of them. To hear their stories, to witness their lives, their loves, their sorrows. She wanted a bond with them beyond crown and countrymen. She wanted to know them, and she wanted them to know her, even if they could never know that it was the heir that walked and danced and sang among them, that drank with their sons, braided their daughters' hair, and dandled their babes on her knees.

No, Abrax would never understand that.

She slipped into the buttery soft billowing pants that laced high on her waist and cinched with pretty, matching embroidered plum ribbons around her ankles. The matching cropped bodice was sleeveless and low cut in the back to accommodate wings.

It was a bit snug, being shop bought and untailored, leaving a sliver of skin exposed between the top of her pants and its bottom hem. But she was satisfied with the look of the whole ensemble. She tied on leather sandals, added a few bangles to her wrists, tied her coin pouch into her pocket, and twisted her hair into a quick coronet braid.

For the finishing touch, she added a woven midnight-blue shawl around her shoulders, and drawing the cowl over her head, she peered into the mirror to make sure everything was in place. Satisfied she could pass as any sphynx woman her age out for the night to celebrate, she slipped out onto the balcony, leaving the doors open to let the night breeze fill her chamber in her absence, and unfurled her wings, letting the light of the full moon caress and illuminate each feather.

Snack will be unhappy if he finds out you're gone, Lyra warned.

Xandrina looked back to where the Tatzelwurm was curled on her bed, a mischievous twist to her lips. *Good.* She stepped up onto the railing and jumped off.

She free-fell for a moment, savoring the swooping sensation that swelled in her stomach and the way the air wrapped around her like the embrace of a friend she'd not seen in quite some time, before pumping her wings and soaring up into the sky. With a soft whoop, she glided over the palace wall momentarily absent of guards as they changed shifts below. She'd been sneaking out since she was old enough to travel alone in the city at night without drawing concerned attention for being out past bedtime. If anyone knew or suspected, they never spoke of it, but she liked to think that they didn't.

She landed in the narrow alley next to her favorite tavern, The Queen's Troth. Laughter and music spilled in equal measure from its open windows along with scents of fresh bread, hearty stews, and grainy ale. She walked in, and a smile immediate and all-consuming spread across her face. The small tavern with its smooth plaster walls and rough-hewn tables was packed, everyone crammed wing tip to wing tip. A group of musicians sat on a low stage against the far wall where a thick-hipped and long-haired sphynx woman sang, her voice carrying over the raucous and rowdy crowd.

The voluptuous barmaid slid her, her usual drink along with a small glass of something stronger with a wink and smile in exchange for a copper coin. Xandrina tapped the small glass on the bar before throwing it back, letting the liquor ignite a fire in her belly before stoking it to an inferno with her usual wine, until she was burning with desire to dance.

The princess shucked her shawl and her sandals before working her way onto the dance floor to join the others. A burly man quickly drew her in, their hips writhing and feet stomping in unison. He trailed his fingers deliciously along her arm as she wrapped it around his neck, making her insides curl contentedly. As one song swelled into another, she shed his company for another's, a buxom beauty with bells on her ankles and beads in her hair. From partner to partner she swayed, snagging shots off the trays of passing barmaids until her heart was pounding, her cheeks were flushed, and her head was in the clouds.

The song shifted, and she pirouetted from the arms of a sweet-faced tradesman into the waiting arms of a soldier. She swallowed thickly as her gaze followed the length of exposed chest, visible through a hastily put on half-unlaced shirt and leather jerkin, up his long-columned neck, to the stubbled jaw of her bonded.

His strange eyes met hers, a smirk on his lips that accentuated a dimple on his cheek she'd somehow missed before that was irritatingly attractive. She pressed her hands to his chest and took a step back while still locked in his embrace. She glared at him, silently daring him to say something, to make a scene, to drag her back to the palace. But he just smiled down at her.

"Well?" she hissed over the melodic din. "Have you come to scold me like a naughty child? To drag me home?"

He brushed a coppery curl off her neck and tucked it behind her ear. He leaned in close so his words were whispered, hot, against the curve of her neck. "I told you, my lady, I will have your back no matter what. I am yours; I am loyal to you. I will follow you anywhere, even if it is to a seedy pub in The Pit."

Abrax cinched his arm around her waist more tightly, drawing her against his chest. "Dance with me, my lady?"

She stared at him a moment, assessing, looking for a hidden trick, then her eyes snagged on a carving of a beautiful woman that was barely hidden against his bronze chest beneath his shirt and a flash of jealousy struck like lightning on the great dunes of the desert, swift and violent. She took the feeling and buried it down deep with all her other discarded emotions she wasn't willing to examine too closely and nodded, allowing him to press her against him.

Their bodies melded, moving as one to the sinuous beat that tied them together, syncing their hips and their heartbeats. As though they were trapped under a spell brewed with liquor and song, their hands roamed each other's bodies. The princess's nose grazed his neck, relishing his intoxicating smell that reminded her of stormy skies and blood-orange sunsets so that she forgot who she was, who he was, and who they were supposed to be together. She imagined that they were two nobodies who met in this bar by chance, that he could sweep her off her feet and take her home to his bed, and that maybe they could build a small but happy life together. But eventually the closing time bell tolled, its echo sliced through her drunken imaginings like an iron ax coming down across her head, and she was instantly sober as she stepped out of her bonded's strong embrace.

They looked at one another then, just briefly before their gazes slid apart, and in stilted silence, the back of her throat coated in bitter shame as she realized just how far she'd let her thoughts stray. As she turned away from him, she loathed him just a little for making her regret, for the first time in her life, the position she'd been born into.

Chapter 21

"No, this way, and we're walking," Xandrina hissed in Abrax's ear as they filtered out of the Queen's Troth with the last dregs of the celebratory crowd. Abrax scowled, but it seemed there was little he could do but comply. The princess was more of a force to be reckoned with than he'd initially expected, not that he was completely sure what it was he'd expected in the first place.

She dragged his arm across her shoulders as if she needed to lean on him for support, blending in with the other stumbling bar patrons as they headed home. Though it was a ruse, he relished the way her skin felt against his, smooth and soft and far more comforting than anything else in his life had been in a very long time.

The narrow, wending road around them slowly emptied, and the distance between lamps stretched out. The night seeped into the gaps, soaking everything in deeper hues. His eyes strained to peer into recessed entryways and down branching alleys to assess for threats.

He bent his head to whisper near the princess's ear, "Where are we?"

She shuddered and shrugged him off as his words wisped across the scant space between them, and something in him that felt too close to his pride shriveled at her spurning. It was ridiculous, he knew, but after hours wrapped in her embrace as they danced, he thought, he thought—no, it didn't matter what he thought.

"Wait here," the princess commanded in a thready murmur, "don't let yourself be seen."

He opened his mouth to protest, his hand outstretched to grab her as she strolled out into an open courtyard that rimmed a giddily splashing fountain. What in the damned Fates was she doing?

That's when Abrax suddenly noticed a shifting shadow on the far side of the square. He was about to step out and shout for the princess to look out, but she shot a glare over her shoulder at him as if she could read him through the bond, but that was impossible with the iron grip she had on it.

"Hello, Mother." Xandrina spoke softly, but in the stillness of the night, her words echoed off the sleeping stone buildings.

Mother? Abrax squinted, trying to make out the face of the person to whom she spoke, but surely, it was not the queen.

She raised her hand as the figure tensed. "I mean you no harm. I simply heard rumor of you and thought to confirm it is all."

There was a pause, swollen and heavy, strung between the princess and the sphynx to whom she spoke, but then it moved, limping forward into a pearlescent shaft of moonlight. Abrax stifled his surprise. It was an old woman, her wings and shoulders drooped and sagging like the edges of a nearly spent candle. In her arms, she held a swaddled bundle.

"What is it ye want from me, Highness?" The woman's words were cracked but not unkind.

"You know me?" Xandrina's surprise was evident in the ruffle of her feathers.

"Aye. I used to work in the palace in my younger years. Ye have grown a bit since the last time I seen ye, though. 'Bout knee high you were then." The woman, the Mother Xandrina had called her, shifted her feet as though it pained her to be on them so long.

The princess shifted, too, a step closer, the tilt of her head assessing. "The kitchens, right? You made those chocolate custard tarts."

The elderly woman's eyes sparkled in the sparce light. "Aye, yes, I did." She paused. "Though I don't have cause or means to bake them much anymore, Highness."

She laughed at that. "No, I don't suppose you would, not with so many mouths to feed."

The bundle in the mother's arms cooed, a small fist stretched up toward the mother's wrinkly face. Not a bundle then, a babe. What was it the princess wanted here, Abrax wondered. Surely, she didn't come all this way for a cook to make her tarts.

"I'm not doing no wrong in taking the babes." Mother tucked her wing protectively, shielding the baby from sight. "The fountain is known, ye see, in the Pit, as a safe place to leave the little ones no one wants. I just make sure they're taken care of is all, teach them their letters and sums when they're old enough. It's not illegal or anything."

It felt as though the night held its breath, waiting for the princess's reply. "Of course, it isn't. That's not why I'm here. I came because I want to help."

Abrax wasn't sure who was more surprised, himself or Mother. "What, what do ye mean, Highness?" Mother's words were spoken so softly they barely reached Abrax's ears.

"I want to provide you with funds and a larger home and even some hired help to assist with the chores. I can hire proper teachers, too. I can get you whatever you need, just say the word." Xandrina was standing directly in front of the elderly sphynx now, brought closer by every word spoken.

Awe smeared with confusion was painted across the Mother's face along with something akin to dawning respect. "Why would ye go through the bother?"

"Because no child should want for anything. Not food or clothes or affection." Those words struck Abrax right in the chest, leaving him breathless and wondering what life would have been like if there had been a Mother and a foundling home like the one the princess dreamed of funding when his mother had passed. If there was, there might have been more than just the cold and brutal embrace of the army to turn to when his belly ached with want of food.

"I would like that very much, Princess, but can ye do it?" Mother asked, her words scrawled all over with tenuous hope.

"I can," she said firmly. Abrax found in that moment that if she said she could pull the moon down from the sky and cut it like cake to feed the hungry, then she could and would do just that.

Chapter 22

Safiya's lady's maid Marryn, despite being given the night off, left her tea tray out and waiting for her return. She sighed with relief as soon as she saw it sitting on the gilded table in front of her empty hearth in the sitting area of her chamber. Though tonight there was one markable difference. There were two cups instead of one. A hint, a gentle nudge to get to know her new bonded. Not that it really mattered if she was to die soon. She sighed resignedly and swept her gaze around her excruciatingly empty chamber. All right, fine, she could give it a try.

"Your rooms are through there." She pointed to the small obscure door near the balcony exit, only noticeable along the muraled walls by the handle that caught the flickering lamp light. "Though perhaps you would like to share a cup of tea with me first, Ocidynus?"

She looked questioningly at her bonded where he lurked near the door. If he were anyone else, she might say he was unsure of himself in that moment, but the man who'd laughed, danced, and fucked women so easily before his trial could surely not feel something so mundane. He was far too cocky to be found on his back foot. Wasn't he?

"Oci." His words came out more growl and grumble than anything else, all rough edges, like a stray that needed caring for. "People who know me call me Oci."

Safiya lowered her hood and unfastened the toggle on the front of her cloak. "Well, Oci, if you would like, I can pour us some tea."

"No." Stubborn, stupid man, they would have to get to know one another at least a little if this was going to work for the time being.

Fine, maybe it wasn't her, maybe it was the tea. He was, after all, quite brutish, handsome, but brutish. "A night cap, then? I have liquor around here somewhere-"

"No." She arched a surprised brow at his harsh rasping tone. He took a step forward, clearing his throat ,and said more softly, a sudden and surprisingly coy curl to his words, that seemed more suited to the rumors she'd heard of him. "I meant I can pour it. While you put away your things." He gestured to the cloak she held.

"Oh well, yes, thank you, that would be lovely." She stood and ducked through the arching doorway to her room and quickly discarded her cloak over a chair. She paused in front of her mirror to run her claws through her scarlet tresses and pinched some color into her cheeks before she returned to what she supposed was to be their shared space from now on. She found Ocidynus—no, Oci, she corrected—waiting in one of the chairs around the table with the tea tray, the two cups already filled and waiting. The delicious scent of the brew's spices drifted through the room.

She sat across from him, letting her wings relax and droop over the back of her seat in a spill of gold and silver feathers. Without waiting to be asked, her bonded passed her a cup on a saucer, the accidental scrape of his calloused fingers along her hand sent goose pimples scurrying up her arm, and for a brief moment, she wondered what it would be like to have those hands wrapped around her waist. But then he bent to pick up his own cup and saucer, and he looked so much like an overgrown child playing with a doll's tea set rather than a man that she had to press her lips tightly together to squash a smile and a laugh.

The queen blew the wafting steam off the creamy nutty-colored drink and took a sip. Oci's aureate eyes bore into her, his breath held waiting for her approval she presumed, his cup half raised to his lips in suspended motion.

She took a sip and stilled. Had she been any other woman, had she been any other queen, she might not have been able to identify the taste in the brew as anything other than someone having a heavy hand with the sweetener. But she wasn't any other woman, and she knew with every aching part of her being that the honey in her cup was not ordinary. It was in fact quite extraordinary, derived from a rare species of bee that lived along the coastline in territory that once belonged to his people, to the alkry. The bee was unique in that its preferred food source was Fates Glory, a deadly dark, night-blooming trumpet flower that crept and crawled on spindly vines all over the cliffs there. In small doses it was pleasant, some even took it for recreation, enjoying the way it made colors and inhibitions bleed. But in larger doses, particularly over a length of time, the toxins in the syrupy golden liquid would build up and cause madness and eventually death. A fact she knew intimately.

Oci watched her, intently, though he was trying to be discreet. He'd remembered to breathe and move again, though his knuckles were white on the handle of his cup. He was doing markedly better than she did the first time she'd slipped a dose to her mother, she had to commend him for that. Though he'd killed before, while her mother was her first, her only, and you never forget your first murder.

She swallowed and let the cup fall to its saucer with a slight chink. She willed her cheeks to pull her lips along into a smile, hoping he couldn't see the coldness she truly felt in the glaze of her eyes. "Wonderful, Oci, thank you. A touch sweeter than I normally take it, but then again, we're celebrating, are we not? So I suppose I can excuse the indulgence." She took another sip, watching as his shoulders relaxed fractionally and the stitch between his brows loosened. Was this it? The means of her death that the dead queen had warned her of? But the dose was small, which meant she likely had time, and she wasn't a novice when it came to ingesting Honey.

"I'll remember that next time, Majesty," he said, a small smirk playing across his full lips, and she had no doubt he would.

She took yet another sip, deliberately locking their gazes as she did. "Please, call me Safiya." It seemed only right for them to be on a first-name basis if he was planning on killing her.

Part
Two

Chapter 23

X andrina whipped her head around at the clattering sound of metal crashing to the floor. "Ugh, could you at least pretend to be competent, Abrax, for Fates' sake?"

"I'm not incompetent," he growled as he stooped to pick up the pair of pauldrons and greaves from the floor. "There's just a lot more to women's armor than my own."

"Ignorance isn't an excuse." She tsked through curled lips, the silver length of her fang kissed her bottom lip in slightly exaggerated irritation. She wasn't half as annoyed as she let on, but if there was anything about him she'd learned in the first fifty days of their bonding, it was that she liked pushing him, trying to see if his cool demeanor would snap. A small irrational part of her wanted to see the man do something other than grumble and grouse. She wanted him to lose his temper completely, to yell at her, to grab her with those large, scarred hands of his, to shake her, to . . .

Abrax held a piece of armor up, catching his reflection in it, and mused, "Do you really need so much gold? It seems a bit impractical."

Xandrina rolled her eyes, grateful he'd interrupted the direction her thoughts had been tilting, and snatched a vambrace from him. "Of course it is impractical, it's ceremonial. Now help me with the buckles on the sides, please." He set the piece down and stooped under her raised arm to buckle her breast plates in place with his careful calloused fingers.

"Isn't it a bit excessive to own gold-plated ceremonial armor?"

"Are you calling me vain?" She raised an eyebrow at him in a way that she knew always made his throat bob, and sure enough, he didn't disappoint.

He swallowed hard, his odd eyes widened just a fraction, the only hint he was caught off guard. "Of course not, no, I, well, what I meant was . . ."

Well, he wasn't mad, but flustered and stammering was the next best thing. "Damn the Fates, Abrax, stop your blathering, we're running late. Grab that trunk"—she gestured to the large bulky box leaning against the wall of her dressing room, one that usually took two servants to handle— "and meet me in the stable yard." She spun and sauntered out, a satisfied feline smirk that he couldn't see on her face and a sway to her hips that she hoped he could.

Chapter 24

"Must you leave us so soon, Cato? It has been such a pleasure to have you with us these past weeks." Safiya clasped her hands neatly in front of her to stop herself from reaching out and hugging the Drakar. They'd had the pleasure of having many a fireside chat with one another over the course of the celebrations, and she'd grown quite fond of the scholar, but as with her daughter, public displays of affection were a sign of weakness and could put a target on anyone's back. And even though Cato lived several Fragments away, she could never be too careful.

His fingers glowed with his magic, making her own itch to be used, as he conjured a door to the void. "As much as I would love to accompany you to present your daughter around your kingdom, I'm sure I could fill tomes about the process and the proceedings, which is quite tempting, I am overdue to head back to Ifris. Perhaps I shall come back another time, and you can regale me with tales of how it unfolds. Over some of that spiced desert plume wine I hope." He winked, his belly shaking with silent laughter.

"That would be wonderful." Safiya smiled, though her heart felt withered and small as he turned to leave. Cato was a true equal, someone with whom she could, at least behind closed doors, relate to without hiding behind a mask, well, not much of one anyway.

The door closed, winking out of existence as if it had never been. She turned, brushed by Oci, who stood just a half step closer than was entirely proper. The backs of their hands slid past one another, sending lightning jolts of warmth shooting up her arm and charging the air around them.

She bit her lip to smother a sigh, crossing the courtyard to mount her horse. She would have much preferred to fly, but many of the members of their entourage were too old, and horses were expected for formal visits. Besides, at this point, there was as much toxin running through her veins as blood, and she never knew when her reality would suddenly tip into hallucination. Oci had been diligent with his doses. True to his word, he remembered she preferred her drinks less sweet, which had bought her some time. But the pleasantly warm feelings she'd felt from the Honey the first few weeks were starting to turn sour. She'd yet to have visions, and the inhibitions she felt were in check, but she needed more time. Time to secure her daughter as heir with the people before her sanity started to fray.

Chapter 25

Safiya enjoyed the ride out of Evernedi. There was a lovely light breeze that lifted the ends of her hair and her feathers as she waved to her people, but the thrill that raced down her spine as soon as they crossed the city threshold couldn't be matched. The maroon sands of the desert sprawled vast and untamable before them with the Pyramid Mountains crowning the distant horizon. The wild was in her blood, in her soul. She loved the empty raw parts of her kingdom nearly as much as she loved her people. Though sometimes it felt like she loved it more just from the longing of it.

"Well now, that's a rare sight," Oci remarked offhandedly from atop his horse next to her.

She couldn't tear her gaze from the view before her as she replied breathily, "It is, isn't it?"

"You mistake me, I didn't mean the landscape, though it is quite beautiful." His deep and rumbling voice scratched at her attention.

Safiya cast a sidelong glance his way, an eyebrow raised at him questioningly. Unconsciously, she prodded the bond between them that had remained sealed tight since their ceremony. "Well, out with it, Oci, I can't read your mind," she quipped, but there was no venom or bite to her words. She was too blissfully happy to see the open road laid bare before her.

"Your smile, Majesty." Oci chuckled darkly, a small smile of his own played at the corner of his wicked lips. "It's the first true one I've seen since bonding with you. I was beginning to think you were unable."

"Are you suggesting I'm dour?" She twisted her face into an overexaggerated grim expression, the kind one might expect to see on the faces of players acting out dramas on stage and not on a queen, but the wild did things to her, lifted her burdens and allowed her to just be.

He laughed, this time a full throaty sound that made her feel inexplicably molten inside. His hard exterior that he'd held closely over his skin since their bonding melted away with that laugh. "Not at all, just that you maybe have forgotten how to be happy."

"My, that is a grim assessment. I might have preferred you think me dour," she quipped playfully, a small part of her hoping to further rub away at his affected persona and find the Oci under it, to see the man beneath.

His raucous laugh filled the air, and she preened like a satisfied kitten at the sound. The heads of the nearest councilmen swiveled in their direction from where they slumped atop their own beasts, but she paid them no heed.

"So you're a shameless flirt, that makes one true thing I know about you then, Oci." That and that he was poisoning her. She snuck a darted glance over at him, keeping her tone light so as not to scare him away. He was a untamed wombellow that had just shown her the slightest bit of attention, but he could still be scared off at the first wrong move.

Curiosity was a nagging fly in her ear whispering all sorts of possibilities about who he was and where he came from. It didn't help that her web of whispers had found next to nothing on him, and he hadn't taken one of her women to bed since the ceremony. Another curiosity.

"Eh well, I wouldn't say I'm shameless, but I have been accused of being a bit flirtatious from time to time." The smirk on his lips suggested otherwise.

Safiya adjusted her reins. "I tell you what, Oci, we have a long journey ahead of us, how about we play a game? A truth for a truth."

He shook his head, his eyes suddenly weighted with an unknowable emotion. "You don't want my truths, Majesty."

Ah, but she did so desperately. She wanted to wring them from him like water from a rag, but trying to pull truths, thoughts, or feelings from him was more akin to trying to squeeze blood from a stone.

"How about a lie for a lie then?" She threw the idea at him as though it had just come to her suddenly, but she'd long known that a person's lies could reveal just as much about them as their truths, sometimes more.

His lips curled back, and he threw back his head and laughed in that way of his again, the way that showed off just the barest sliver of his soul. "Now that sounds like my kind of game."

Chapter 26

Abrax heaved a weary sigh of relief when the lights of the oasis village came into view. He'd been on the edge of a knife the whole ride, his teeth gritted, ever wary of some potential threat to his princess. Some might call it impractical, his ever-present vigilance, but after what happened to his mother, it was not something he could lose his grip on. He could never lose his temper, he could never slip. If he did, it could cost him everything . . . it could cost him the princess.

After the past several weeks as her silent stalking shadow, he was convinced she was Gypette's salvation. Her mother's aim for peace between the former valkry nation and the sphynx kingdom was all well and good, but he believed that for there to be peace and well-being among all, it would come from her with her relentless determination, cunning, and compassion for her people.

He'd admittedly thought her a reckless and spoiled brat when she'd sneaked out to go dancing, but then he realized that while, yes, dancing and drinking was a part of it, getting to know her people and hearing their concerns was her foremost priority. A fierce burning had sparked to life in his chest during that first council meeting when she'd advocated for revenue to be allocated to fund a foundling house in the Pit after meeting Mother on that first night he'd followed her.

The council, of course, pushed against it at first, but she wouldn't be swayed. She walked straight out of that meeting with a determination in her step that could have crumbled walls. She went straight to her closet and put on a flimsy gauzy dress that would have made a courtesan blush. At that night's feast, she'd danced with every single available male descendant of those council members that opposed her. She even let one dandle her on his knee in the dark recesses of the balcony, crooning in his ear and running her claws through his hair as he nibbled her neck and wrapped his meaty hands around her slender waist. Abrax had the barely suppressible urge to rip them from his body and nail them to the council chamber door. It was like wrestling a beast, but he managed to subdue and stuff the ridiculously violent notion down deep and bury it. The vote on the funding passed during the next session, and Mother had the gold and a crew of builders to construct a fine home for her and her younglings before the week's end.

Their procession passed through a roughly stacked stone arch that framed the reflection of the setting sun across the oasis as if it were a painting. The village was little more than a tent city with very few permanent structures aside from a large stone meeting hall with a thatched roof and a trading post. It was still grander than his humble beginnings, though.

"Come back from your daydream, bonded, and make sure my tent gets set up, would you? I don't want to sleep in the sand." The princess slid from her horse as soon as the group halted, rolling her shoulders and stretching her wings wide to catch the sun's glittering light along the silver and gold of her feather tips.

Abrax dismounted and dusted the desert off his leathers. "You have servants for that, my lady. I'm not your errand boy." She was forever trying to push him, and while he would lay the fragment at her feet or pluck the stars from the sky for her to wear as jewels should she ever ask, sometimes he liked watching the way she squirmed when he denied her.

When she whipped her head around, he expected to see a thunderhead in her eyes; instead, she just narrowed her gaze slightly and shrugged her shoulders. "Suit yourself, but if they do it wrong, don't come complaining to me when you have sand flea bites on your ass."

He choked on a laugh as she sauntered off with an irritatingly hypnotic sway to her hips. He quickly cleared his throat and trained his eyes on the point of her back where her wings protruded and followed her as she fell in line behind her mother and Oci to greet the village elders. This was going to be a long trip.

Chapter 27

Safiya accepted the gracious hands of the elders before letting them lead her into the dimly lit meeting house with its hard-packed floors and rows of dusty benches. Yarressa, the oldest member of the tribes council whose face had long since been weathered by the sands, pulled her aside before she could make it to the front with a wrinkled hand on her elbow. "Begging your pardon, Majesty, but I have some news I'd like to discuss with you that I think is best heard outside of the meeting hall. It is of a disturbing nature, and I don't wish to alarm the people, nor take the stage away from your lovely daughter."

The queen furrowed her brow. It was not like Yarressa to be so cloak and dagger; worry swam in her milky eyes that sent a shock of concern through Safiya's heart. Whatever it was that the elder wanted to tell her would be dark indeed. She patted the older woman's hand. "Come to my tent this evening, we'll have tea and discuss it then."

The hall filled quickly as the hammered bell that hung in its modest belfry was tolled to signal their arrival to the whole of the oasis. Safiya and Xandrina waited in stilted silence as the tribe's folk filtered in, the elders and leaders taking the front rows followed by the younger and sturdier of wing and back. She recognized many faces among them from her visits over the years, though the time since her last visit showed on everyone's faces. A trade runner near the back, Harell, whom she'd met when she was first crowned, had been but an apprentice to his father, and now he stood with his arm wrapped around a sphynx woman with a swollen belly and a toddler on her hip. Safiya kept the small smile that itched to pull at her lips subdued.

When all had at last assembled, the most wizened of the elders stood with the help of a knotted cane, his shoulders stooped under the weight of his wings, and raised a chipped clawed hand to silence the murmuring that ran through the room. He then bowed so stiffly Safiya wished she could reach out and assist him as he nearly fell back along his bench. Fortunately, a younger sphynx behind him had the same idea and caught him by the elbow as he began to teeter and assisted him back into his seat.

The queen stepped forward, the tribal elders' actions giving her the floor. She centered herself on the packed floor between the aisles in the last rosy, golden shaft of sun that reached its way in through the meeting hall's entry. Beyond it through the rippling haze of heat that stubbornly clung to the day, she saw the waiting faces of the crowd outside, their ears craned to hear her. Before she could open her mouth, an unexpected and ill-timed wash of fever poured a cold and dreadful sweat down her back.

She swallowed, her throat suddenly coated in thick, acrid bile. Safiya forced a smile and pressed her hands into her belly to hold her nerves steady. She cut a glance to where Oci leaned against the wall, seemingly indolent and lethal at the same time. Did he know his poison was working its will on her already? Could he see it in the pale of her skin? No, she could not think of that now. Her daughter, she had to present her daughter.

"Thank you all for assembling today," her voice echoed back to her, redoubling in her ears so it thrummed around her skull and grew in pitch until it felt as though her every word were being screamed at her. "My daughter, the Princess Xandrina Astarte Narsissa, descendant of the great Traveler Inana Ishtar and bearer of her magic, stands before you now, having triumphed over her fears. She and I would like to humbly beg for your acceptance of her as the heir to the throne of our great lands."

Chapter 28

As was custom, Xandrina and her mother both knelt and held their hands up like beggars in the Pit asking for alms. The granules of sand not swept from the floor dug into the princess's knees with all the bite of shards of glass, but she thought, at least, that she managed to keep the wince off her face as the anxiety surging in her blood played with her nerves like a kitten was wont to do with string.

"We beg on our knees, great people of the sand, forged of fire and wind, that you will accept my heir as your own as you once accepted me," her mother intoned.

Following her mother's lead, Xandrina lowered herself to the ground further until she lay prostrate before the people, her forehead kissing the ground, and waited. There was a pause, each drawn-out moment punctuated by the thundering of Xandrina's heart across her ribs as she waited for the people to come forward. Would they accept her? Or would she be the first heir in history to be rejected? Her blood roared in her ears so loudly she was sure that it must be loud enough for all to hear and to witness. The knot that was her bonded throbbed in the back of her head, tempting her to reach out to him for comfort.

Calm yourself, pet, be as still as stone. They will accept you just as I did. Lyra's hissed words cut through the thunderous rumble of her heart like an eye in a storm giving a brief reprieve. *Besides, most of them are quite old and feeble, it will take them a moment to get their decrepit bones moving. Oh, look, I think that one is sleeping; there's drool leaking out of its maw.*

Xandrina held her breath, the wave of nerves metamorphosizing into the urge to giggle uncontrollably. *Stop it, you're going to make me laugh, and then they definitely won't accept me,* the princess chided the wurm. *And thank you.*

Lyra purred just as Xandrina felt the first of her people come forth, the edge of their robes brushing against her splayed hands, and then one by one the tribesmen all came and bestowed their allegiance, acceptance and favor upon her. She knew from stories told to her by Glendora that the favors would range in magnitude from small, polished pebbles to yards of hand-dyed silk, to curved blades set with desert stones and etched in runes meant to bring the Fate of Luck to the wielder's hand.

Her mouth tasted of dirt and sand and spent emotions. Her muscles began to ache, straining against her bones so tightly she feared they might snap if she had to hold the bow one minute longer, and then with the sound of drums and a whoop of celebration from somewhere outside the meeting house, the ceremony ended.

Slowly, she pushed herself up, her joints protesting and popping angrily. Blinking in the low light, she took in the array around her where the gifts of the people lay like an oddly patterned mandala. She met her mother's gaze, something in them looked painfully like sympathy, and it was only then that she realized her own eyes were rimmed in the silver of unshed tears, lids heavy with the weight of expectation and responsibility to the people. It was almost as much of a burden as the crowning had been, maybe more, and she felt it all pressing in on her, squeezing her in its fist.

Safiya came to her then, perhaps emboldened by the lack of eyes currently watching them, leaned down, and placed a kiss upon the coppery crown of Xandrina's head. "You made me proud today, daughter." The words were whispered like a deathbed confession, so faint that Xandrina wasn't certain she heard her correctly. Then her mother swept from the meeting house and into the night, leaving her alone with her bonded.

Chapter 29

Abrax watched as the sparks from the bonfire pirouetted into the sky as though their greatest wish was to join the stars that shimmered there, illuminating the crushing black of night. Xandrina danced around the fire, dressed in tribal-style silks tediously woven from the cocoons of the luminary moths that nested in the berry brush that only grew around the sacred waters of the oasis. They produced the softest and the most durable fabric in the kingdom; selling a single bolt of the stuff could bring a very tidy sum. The princess's skirt flowed like water off her hips with near scandalous slits up the sides and a barely there bodice that left the full length of her back exposed.

He watched the fabric slip luxuriously across her skin, catching the firelight and making it look like she was dressed in golden moonlight. He stood stiffly on the fringes of the gathering, keeping an eye on every angle of the party with the empty night desert at his back. A lone sentinel.

Oci slipped out of the darkness on silent feet, appearing next to him. Oci was the only sphynx he knew who could sneak up on him, though he'd grown used to it over the years to the point that him materializing out of thin air no longer quickened his pulse or sent his hand fluttering to his knife hilt. "She's off-limits you know, Mutt."

Abrax glanced at him sidelong. "I'm just watching my charge as you should be."

"The queen's tent is still within eyesight." He took an appallingly large swig from his mug, the stench of sour ale thick in the air when he spoke.

Abrax crossed his arms and continued to map the princess's movements as she tumbled from the arms of one dance partner to the next. Their hands on her made him want to grind his teeth; any one of them could have a hidden knife or a vial of poison. Or she might take one of them to *play* back at her tent, which was somehow infinitely worse.

"See? That's what I mean, you're in love with the bloody girl, aren't you, Mutt? It'd be best to go find yourself a nice concubine to release your woes, boy. The likes of them are not for the likes of us."

Abrax growled and grabbed the mug from Oci's hand. He threw it back, downing it all in one gulp, and shoved it into the older man's chest hard enough to make him stumble backward. "You have no idea what you're talking about, Oci."

But the valkry just laughed at his back as Abrax stalked stubbornly away.

Chapter 30

Safiya slid into her night dress and robe on her own, she had only a small retinue of servants with her, many of whom were a part of her inner circle, her web of whispers. She needed their eyes and ears out there among the milling crowds where they could pick up useful tidbits of information, not in her tent tending to simple needs she could see to herself. The reception had gone better than she could have ever dreamed. Not that there was typically much dissent in the tribes. Their bags of gold never ran dry as they were the main source of trade throughout the kingdom and were kept well employed by the crown. They kept well away from court politics besides.

"Majesty." Yarressa slipped in through the back of Safiya's tent like a whisper.

The elder woman made as if to bow before where Safiya was seated by a low fire with a lantern burning and a book on her lap, but the queen stood, took the woman by the elbow and steered her into a chair opposite hers by the warmth of the hearth. The desert night's chill was fast approaching, riding the back of a slow breeze. "Come sit with me, Yarressa, there is no need to stand on formalities in private. What news you have?"

The older woman wrung her thick silvering braid between both hands, and her eyes darted to the shadowy corners of the tent with such fear that it was as though she expected them to swell and swallow her whole. "There have been rumors of beasts stalking the caravans, Majesty. Many of the chattel have gone missing on the darkest of the nights. Two of my best drivers have come forward, mind you, these are both sensible fellows, they don't take to drinking or telling tall tales, but they both say they've seen odd tracks in the desert the likes of which they've never seen before. The sort that have long claws."

Safiya furrowed her brow and steepled her fingers beneath her chin thoughtfully. "Have these men traded along the coasts before, in the old valkry lands?"

Yarressa shook her head. "You're thinking it's harpies coming inland, my Queen, but I assure you my men know when they've seen harpies. Both have been with me for many seasons and have run many a trade route, even ones by the sea, they know the difference between those bitches"—she spat on the floor— "and beasts."

"And they were well watered and fed?" Safiya raised her hands placatingly as the woman began to squawk indignantly. "I know you know how to care for your folk, Yarressa. I just need to consider all possibilities, and we both know the sands like to play tricks on the mind from time to time on the weak and overweary."

"You said it yourself; I know how to care for my men, they are both hale, healthy, and have their wits about them. There is one more thing further that I haven't mentioned." She crossed her arms beneath her shawl, drawing it in around herself. The queen gestured for her to go on. "They both said that whatever is lurking doesn't seem like a normal beast, they say it feels wrong, and it's far too clever. The chattel that were taken, Majesty, they were untied from their lines not just grabbed or cut free, and there wasn't a single drop of blood or tuft of hair left behind save for the claw marks in the sand."

The queen tapped her talons on the leather-bound cover of her book. "That is concerning indeed, Yarressa. I appreciate you coming to me with this. I'll tell my guards to keep extra eyes on the sands as we travel, and I'll send an extra reserve of coin for you and the other tribes to hire more men to ensure the safety of the caravans."

"Thank you, Majesty, that is much appreciated." The old woman stood and pulled the cowl of her shawl over her salted-silver hair, shadowing her face.

"One more thing, Yarressa." The old woman paused in her leaving and nodded to show she was listening. "Send word to me directly should there be any further developments, any sightings, or if anything or anyone else goes missing."

Yarressa bobbed a half a bow. "As you wish, my Queen. Sleep well and Fates bless you." Then she slipped back out into the night as quietly as she'd come. In the brief silence that followed, it was almost as if she'd never been there except for the aching sense of foreboding that sat like a maelstrom in Safiya's stomach.

When Safiya tried to sleep that night, she dreamed of claws ripping through the velvety dark.

Chapter 31

Xandrina could feel his eyes on her through the night tracing her steps like an extra shadow, circling the fire like a carrion bird waiting for its next meal. It was a comfort. It was torture. She truly would never be free of this push and pull, this swell of knotted feelings in her head that she had to be wary of at all times.

Come to bed, pet, your thoughts are soaked in booze and making my head spin, Lyrahvi hissed through her mind, her annoyance a near tangible taste in Xandrina's mouth.

But she didn't want to come to bed, she wanted to dance with enough men and woman that her bonded's tightly leashed self-control snapped. She wanted him to be the one to pull her into his arms and press his body close, to trail his fingers along her bare skin. She wanted to lean in and savor the smell of him; she wanted to be so undone by him as she had been on that first night of the Fifty Feasts that she questioned the entirety of her world.

I said come to bed, pet. The command in Lyra's words as they hissed through her mind startled her enough to stumble. The sand rushed up to meet her, but a firm grip on her elbow pulled her back. Arms encircled her, cocooning her in that too familiar smell.

"I have your back." His words crashed into her, falling through the cage of her ribs to settle in her core where they pulsed wickedly. She twisted petulantly out of his arms, embarrassment crawling up her cheeks. Fates, she couldn't want this man.

"I'm fine," she spat, though her words may have slipped and slurred into one another, she couldn't quite be sure. "I just need to . . ." Damn him, but he was smiling at her. It was small, but it was there, and it only made that pulsing within her ache more deeply.

"What is it that you need, Princess?" he asked, his voice dangerously low as he took a step closer. The firelight smoldered in his two-toned gaze. Her lower lip quavered, her tongue caught halfway between telling him she needed him and only him and telling him she just needed sleep.

Something unreadable flickered across his face, and suddenly the blazing heat that was in his eyes a moment before was doused. He took her arm, but there was nothing in the touch that made her insides curl. "Come, let's get you to bed."

Xandrina's lower lip pouted, and she was about to protest when the flash of a leathery wing caught the corner of her gaze. She swiveled her head to look back over her shoulder as Abrax pulled her toward the tent to find her mother's bonded slipping into the shadows, a devious and far too knowing look on his face.

Her insides twined in an altogether unpleasant manner. What had he seen? What would he say to her mother? She tried to calm her thoughts that spiraled out of control as they ducked into their shared tent, and she twisted from his grasp to stumble for her bed. There was nothing for the valkry to see; there was nothing for him to tell. There had been no lines crossed between her and Abrax, but as her head hit the pillow, she realized she wanted to dance across every single one of them, consequences be damned.

Chapter 32

Oci's head buzzed pleasantly with ale and secrets as he staggered into his shared tent with the queen. The light of the dying embers from the bonfire danced as sinuously as the tribeswomen against the canvas walls, lighting his way across the carpeted floor.

In the bed, the queen thrashed, battling sheets twisted around wing and limb. A whimper slipped from her lips and stirred up an unfortunate tempest of lust within him. He leaned against the bedpost at the foot of her bed and watched as she rolled, her hips swelling beneath the sheet, her scarlet hair coming unbound.

She bolted awake, her breaths heaving her breasts along the top hem of her nightdress, and she bit off a small, strangled scream as she lunged, her talons lengthened, for his throat. He let her, holding perfectly still as she blinked up at him through sleep-hazed eyes, the razor-sharp points of her claws dimpling his skin. "Oh," she whispered, "it's just you."

Oci's lips curled. "Just me." He affixed his eyes on hers, using every ounce of his will not to stare down at the way her slip of a nightdress hugged her body. He raised an eyebrow at her. "Not that I don't love your hands on my body, but unless you're planning to rip out my throat, I might breathe easier if you remove your claws from it." He kept his tone light and teasing, but there was a sharp edge inside of his mind that cut through his intoxicated lust that said she might do just that if she knew the truth of what he was doing to her, of what he had planned.

He could barely see in the dim flickering light as her cheeks flamed. She let her hand drop before wriggling her way back to the head of her bed and shimmying below her sheet once again. He could feel the whispered ghost of her skin against his, but he cleared his throat and did his best to shove the feeling away. "Bad dreams, Your Majesty?"

"Something like that," she murmured as she began to rebraid her hair.

"Want a bedtime story to help you sleep?" The words were out of his mouth before he could stop them, Fates be fucked, he must be drunker than he thought.

But she laughed, clear as a bell, the sound ringing around his heart. "A story? From you?" she said incredulously.

"Yes, from me." He invited himself to sit on the edge of her bed and kicked his feet up so he could lean against the bedpost lackadaisically and face her. "I had a mother once upon a time, you know, one who told me tales to help me sleep."

"Did you now? And here I thought you spawned out of the desert sands." She was teasing, but he saw something like curiosity flicker in her golden gaze.

"Yes well, don't go spreading it around, I wouldn't want the other soldiers getting the wrong idea. It might ruin my reputation."

"Well, I suppose that depends," she teased, her eyes crinkling at the corners.

"On what?" Oci let his feet fall and scootched closer, so he was nearly even with where she sat propped against her bevy of bolsters and pillows.

She leaned in, tightening the gap between them until she was stealing his breath. "On how good the story is."

"Well, all right, let's see." Oci rubbed the stubble on his chin thoughtfully, swallowing hard around the lump of desire lodged in his throat that begged him to lean in and taste her. "A story fit for a queen . . . Once upon a time, across the scarlet sands in the old kingdom of the valkry, there lived a princess. She was more beautiful than any who'd come before her, with wings the color of night to match her hair and eyes that could see into a man's soul."

"I like her already." The queen smiled coyly, looking up at him through long lashes as she slid down letting her head settle on the pillow.

"No more interruptions or you'll ruin the story." Oci tsked before continuing. "The princess's father was elderly, and he knew his days were numbered. His dearest wish was to see his daughter happily married, so when he was gone, she would have a king to care for and support her, much like he and his wife had had one another for all their years. But his daughter was a force to be reckoned with, and she would not have just any valkry to wed. No matter how many noble sons her father trotted out before her to preen and praise her for her wit and beauty or to charm her with their good looks and impressive wingspans, she refused to bat a flirtatious eye at any of them.

"After weeks of trying to find his daughter a suitable match, the king was growing quite weary and threatened to match her with the next noble son to ask. As I'm sure you can imagine, the princess liked that not at all, but she had duties to attend to that she could not shirk. You see once every few days, the princess would hear the plights of the people, of prisoners, of visiting dignitaries, of basically anyone who showed up at the palace to ask. On that particular day, a prisoner arrived. He was the last to be seen, hauled in by a guard with iron binding his hands. When asked what it was he came to petition her for, he wove for her the tale of his arrest. He explained that there was a hungry child in the market, recently orphaned and trying to fend for herself; she'd tried to steal a loaf of bread to fill her and her younger brother's starving bellies when she'd been caught. The baker, apparently a notoriously ruthless man, grabbed the girl and threatened to ask the magistrate for the harshest possible punishment for her when the man stepped in and took the girl's place. He argued that poverty and hunger were not crimes, that the girl was too young and frightened to know where to seek proper help. But when he came to the end of his story, the princess was left aghast when he begged, not to be pardoned or freed, but for the princess to send aid to the girl and her brother to make sure they were safe and fed."

"It was then that the princess ordered him freed. She sent away his guard and ordered a servant to fetch a bowl of water. When it came, the princess ordered the man to sit on her throne where she washed his face and tended to the wounds he'd sustained while being arrested and imprisoned. As she did so, the princess spoke to him of how his kindness awed her and how their kingdom was sorely in need of his brand of compassion. When she was finished, and he was clean, she got on her knees before him and begged him to ask her father for her hand in marriage, to be her king, but more importantly, to help her rule their kingdom with the same love and sacrifice that he'd showed for the child.

"Awed by her words, he humbly accepted. When he went to her father the king at first, he refused; the man was, after all, of common birth, a mere fisherman. But then the princess explained that in action and deed he was far more noble than any valkry that had asked for her hand before. She then reminded him of his oath to marry her off to the next noble man who asked, and at last seeing not only reason, but the blossoming affection for the man in his daughter's eyes, he relented and blessed the engagement.

"The two were quickly married, giving her father his dying wish for her to have someone to care for her and support her, and together they loved not only each other, but also their people. And there was peace and prosperity for their reign."

Silence stretched between them as he finished his story with Safiya looking up at him sleepily as though he were a piece of a puzzle that she couldn't quite make fit despite it being the only one remaining. "What were their names? This king and queen?" she whispered.

He shifted uncomfortably on the edge of the bed. "They have none; they're just a story."

She hummed a faint reply, her words muttered so softly he couldn't make them out as her eyes were pulled closed, heavy with exhaustion.

Oci watched her for a few moments longer than he should have, as her breaths were drawn long and deep. The drink that had been addling his thoughts now whittled at the edges of his skull, causing it to ache and the room to tilt. Eventually he stood when he was sure the queen was sleeping soundly and stumbled to his pallet, neatly laid out behind a woven screen on the far side of the tent.

He shucked off his boots and his clothes before flopping down on top of the blankets with a grunt, not bothering to fumble his way beneath them. As his eyes slid closed for the night, their names fluttered through his thoughts—Jezzamine and Farin the greatest monarchs in valkry history, but to him they had always just been Mom and Dad.

Chapter 33

Safiya rose before the sun, dressed herself, and strolled out among the camp. She followed her nose to the nearest cook cart where a stringy old sphynx man with milky eyes was brewing the morning tea for the workers and the soldiers, passing it out in tin cups. She slipped in line, the hour still dark enough that none recognized her. With her cowl up, even though her clothes were of fine make, she could have been any one of the many courtesans or mistresses traveling with the procession. Councilmen couldn't be expected to go too long without dipping their wicks after all.

She skirted the edge of the wagons and slipped out into the open desert. She really should have a chat with her general about having such vast gaps in their perimeter, but right then she didn't care if it allowed her a moment's peace. Besides, even if there were beasts lurking in the sands, she had magic. She found a small footpath worn between low-growing scrub brush dappled with pinhead-sized fragrant white blooms and followed it to the crest of a squat dune overlooking the oasis at her back and the vast open desert at her front. She settled onto the ground in a splay of skirts and tossed back the hood of her cloak to allow the morning breeze to kiss her cheeks. The sun showed only the barest hint that it might be ready to roll out of bed and tumble over the horizon as it stretched out its first rays of magenta light.

The tin-cup tea tasted blissfully bitter without even the slightest hint of sweetness. It gave her a giddy jolt to think that she'd found her way around having Oci prepare her morning tea as he so often did. She took another sip, this one deeper, savoring each drop. It tasted like moments of her life being put back on the clock that counted down to the inevitable.

"Trying to give me the slip, Majesty?" She bit her tongue to stifle a groan, before casting her glance around to find her bonded striding across the rise, his shirt only half done, his sleeves rolled to his elbow with one hand resting on the hilt of his sword. His hair was loose, drifting across his shoulders in the same breeze that greeted her. His face, though wearing his usual mask of flirtation, also carried that slice of vulnerability she'd seen the night before when he'd spun for her stories of kings and queens to help her sleep, if you knew where to look.

She smiled tightly. She couldn't have him thinking even in jest that she was intentionally trying to avoid him, as that could raise too many suspicions, and more importantly, then she might not be able to get away with it again. "I wouldn't dare." She patted the sand next to her. "Come watch the sunrise with me." She turned back to look at the pinkening horizon, strangely self-conscious about the invitation. She didn't want to have to look him in the eye if he rejected it.

He made very little sound as he settled next to her cross-legged as she was, close enough that their knees almost brushed. Safiya pressed her lips into a thin line to stop herself from smiling and took another sip of her tea. The bitterness was a slap to the face, a reminder that she was in fact out here to avoid him and his Honey.

He nudged her lightly with an elbow, and she glanced down. Between his thumb and forefinger was pressed the tiniest bouquet of white flowers. "Beautiful flowers for a beautiful flower," he offered with a teasing grin.

Safiya couldn't help herself. She laughed and took them. "It's no wonder you have all the women sighing in your wake with words as sweet as that." It was his turn to laugh, deep and throaty, as she tucked the cluster of blooms behind her ear.

"Oh, Majesty, my words aren't the only thing about me that leaves them sighing." He winked rakishly.

She rolled her eyes and guffawed. "You're so swollen with confidence, Oci, it's a wonder your horse can even carry you."

"That's not the only thing that—" Safiya cut him off with a light shove.

"Don't you dare!" she gasped in mock horror.

Oci held up his hands in playful defeat. "All right, all right, you're right, Majesty. Let us talk of more appropriate things. Let's see, what's on the itinerary for today? Listening to nobles pander or allowing the councilmen to kiss your boots."

The queen rolled her eyes, but she did it with a smile still tugging at the corners of her mouth. "No pandering or boot kissing until this evening, once the caravan has moved, but today we are scheduled to take a small party and detour to collect taxes. Then I believe we are expected to take a tour of some of the mines in the area."

Ocidynus went utterly still next to her. She peered at him sidelong from beneath her lashes, disguising the movement by taking the last drink of her tea. He was pale, so pale for a moment she thought to reach out to him with her magic to see if he needed healing, and then it struck her. What a fool she was to not have thought of it before. He was valkry, and in all likelihood he'd been in those mines, and if not the one they were meant to visit, then one very like it.

"Very well, Majesty, shall I go prepare the horses then?" he ground out through gritted teeth, but he wasn't looking at her, he was looking into some distant and horrible past, his golden eyes dark with the haunting memory as he shot to his feet.

She stood only a moment after him, but he was already turning to leave when she touched him lightly on the elbow, the slowly rising sun alighting on every scar along his forearm. She was astounded there were so many. How was it that she'd never taken notice? She swallowed hard, summoning her voice from where it seemed choked behind some unnamable emotion lodged in her throat. "On second thought, that is a lot of riding for one day. Have a servant send word to the princess that today we will divide and conquer. She will go to the mines in my stead, and we shall go to collect the taxes ourselves."

He stared at the place where her hand rested on his skin before he flicked his eyes up to meet her gaze with something almost questioning swimming in it. Suddenly self-conscious, she drew her hand back.

There was a pause that lasted only a few quick stuttering heartbeats as they looked at one another, but it felt as though it drew itself out into the full length of a day. Safiya didn't want to be the one to remove her gaze first, so instead, she nodded toward the path. "Better get going if we're to be back in time for boot-licking hour."

His lips curled deliciously as he leaned into the space between them. "Kissing."

Her heart fumbled and crashed into her ribs. Fates, why was he talking about kissing all of a sudden? She'd been looking at his lips, but surely he didn't think she meant . . . "What?"

"It's boot-kissing hour, not licking, though I'd pay a pretty bit to see them lick your boots too." He chuckled, and it filled some of the emptiness in his eyes.

She choked on a laugh. "Right, yes well, better ready those horses. I'll be right behind you."

He threw another one of those winks of his over his shoulder as he strode for the top of the path. "I know you will."

Chapter 34

Xandrina was not pleased with her mother demanding she accompany the councilmen on a tour of the mines. The day was scorching, the winds too still, and the councilmen droned as incessantly as the biting black-winged insects that flitted around her ears. Now that she thought on it, she might have preferred the insects. The tour had to end soon; they'd strolled past every building and dismal shack constructed along the scraggly hillside. They'd listened to a lecture on the tailings pile, perused the sorting areas where miners gave each haul brought up a rough going over, plucking the gems and minerals they thought were of the most value and sorting them into barrels to be carted to another camp for further inspection and processing. This particular mine was supposedly filled with the highest quality blood opals and rubies, a fact that the bespectacled overseer never failed to point out every time he opened his mouth.

"We have just this morning uncovered a vein deep within the seventh sector. Our initial inspections suggest it could produce a substantial yield." The overseer's nasally words caused a stir among the cluster of council members.

The princess leaned into Abrax, and whispered with an eyeroll, "Right, how convenient that such a discovery was made on the morning of the royal visit."

Abrax's lips curled, and his strange two-tone eyes glinted with mischief as he looked back at her. "The Fate of Fortune must have blessed the mine herself."

Xandrina pressed her lips into a thin line to seal in a laugh, but then Councilman Fayden piped up over the rest of the balding men. "The princess is right, how do we know this supposed discovery isn't a ruse to coerce us into investing in a worthless endeavor? For all we know, your mine is as dried up as an old wombellow tit."

Fates be damned, she must have spoken louder than she thought, and now the idea was spreading like fire over spilled oil, shouts of take *us into the mines* and *let us see for ourselves* were be brandished in the overseer's face. He held his hands up placatingly. "Highness, your eminences, please, it would be my honor to show you the vein in question. If you could just follow me this way, it would be no trouble. Then you will see that the Fates truly have blessed our operation."

The sphynx started guiding their group toward a gaping, jagged slash in the rockface that looked to her like a sideways wicked grin, and she blanched. She swallowed hard and forced her feet to keep an even, steady pace, though everything in her screamed to turn around. Creatures with wings were not meant to be underground; it was unnatural. They needed air and sun and wind; she needed those things.

As they began the short ascent to the entrance, Fayden leaned in, and whispered conspiratorially in her ear, "What an excellent plan, Your Highness. Of course, I myself was just about to suggest the same when you spoke—" The rest of his oily words slid away as the maw of the mine loomed above them, opening wide to swallow them into its dark and dank depths.

As if sensing her unease, Abrax offered her an arm, which she took gratefully as the greasy councilman slipped away to vie for a spot next to their guide. She sucked in a breath as they stepped over the threshold. The air around them changed immediately, the heat of the day replaced with a bone-chilling cold, the kind of cold she imagined only the dead felt as they lay upon their stone slabs for viewing before their final funeral rites were administered.

Xandrina tried to breathe out, but her lungs stuck, clinging for dear life against her ribs. A scream grew in the base of her throat, as each sloping step brought them further, deeper into the mine, trying to claw its way out. She ground her teeth to cage it—she couldn't scream, she couldn't whimper, she couldn't so much as flutter an eyelash wrong with the council members so nearby. She had to be strong; she had to be unyielding. She had to be the crown in her mother's stead.

She looked back toward the entry, the sliver of light there as slight as the shine of a single star. How had they come so far so fast? The lanterns filled with flickering flame strung along the wall at irregular intervals seemed to flounder in the face of the crushing and consuming black. Her vision shuttered, and her head felt altogether too light and airy.

"Breathe, Princess." Abrax's whispered words caressed the shell of her ear. "Let it out." As if his words held more command over her body than her thoughts did, her lungs complied. "Now back in again- and out."

Something wet pooled under her palm, and she looked down to where her hand rested on her bonded's arm. Her talons had penetrated the leather of his jerkin and apparently his flesh. Her eyes widened in horror. She had to get a grip. She made to pull her hand away, but he simply covered it with his. "It's fine." His words were low and rasped. "I've had worse. Besides, I know someone who can do some exceptional healing with magic." He smiled at her softly, but it didn't soothe the guilt that she'd inflicted real pain upon him when he'd so obviously had much of it in his life.

She was about to apologize when he cut her off. "My mother wasn't fond of dark, closed in spaces either," he said in hushed tones as he slowed their steps, so their group carried on ahead of them out of earshot. "She was a valkry taken by the army in conquest on one of their raids. They, well, they were not kind. She had many fears that clung to her from those times before she was freed. I-"

She thought she saw his cheeks pinken slightly in the dark, and he coughed to cover it up.

"I used to sing to her when she was overcome."

"And what of your father?" Xandrina asked. "What did he do to help when she was afflicted?"

The embarrassment on his face deepened, and his words came out in a barely audible rasp. "There was no father, none she felt worth mentioning beyond the fact that he was a sphynx in the queen's army of some rank, and I've never sought to find him."

There was a look on his face that made her want to comfort him as her mind reeled in search of words, but all she managed was a blurted, "I don't have a father either."

That made him chuckle, then his blue and golden eyes met hers. "Yes, I know, the royal line is conceived with magic, right? No males needed."

It was her turn to burn with mortification. "Yes, well, I suppose that isn't a secret. Still, I see other families when I take my trips into the Pit, and sometimes I wonder what it would be like to have been raised that way, with two loving parents. I'm sorry, I know I sound silly, poor spoiled princess." She laughed self-deprecatingly.

"No, don't do that." He drew her up short, tugging her aside into a small hollow laced through with the luminescent scarlet threads of blood opal. "It's okay to mourn the life you wished you had, no matter your station. I know, I know the royal family is wealthy, but there are other kinds of abundance. Until sickness took my mother, I grew up in a home run on a meager wage, but it was overflowing with love, and that more than made up for what we lacked."

Their heads were bent close, eyes locked on one another, and she was suddenly aware of how near to each other they stood in the nook, of how there was an emotion she couldn't quite name spiraling in the depths of his gaze that made her blood tingle like she'd had too much wine.

She snapped the tension that seemed to be weaving between them like spider silk by summoning a thread of magic to heal his wounded arm. "I know what you're doing, distracting me." She dared a glance up at him again through her lashes as the magic finished knitting his skin. "Thank you."

She turned to pull out of the safety of their little cavern, to rejoin the group, when Abrax took her by surprise, he grabbed her chin in his gentle fingers and turned her to look at him. For an explosive moment, she thought he might kiss her, but he spoke instead. "You are the fiercest and most powerful creature in any room you walk into. Never forget it."

As he stepped out into the mine shaft and offered her his arm once again so they could continue on, Xandrina told herself the sinking sensation in her belly had more to do with her lingering fears rather than disappointment, but she knew it was a lie.

Chapter 35

Oci's knuckles were white, gripped on the reins of his horse as they trotted through the dense forest, the dark shadows of night still curled sleepily under the base of the trees despite the hour. He eyed the thick, twisting patches of shadow as if they harbored his darkest secrets.

Oci, do not fret, we'll make your dreams come true.
The vengeance you seek we can give to you.
Time and patience are thin.
Whisper to us on the wind when it is time to begin.

The branches rustled with the murmuring memories of the voice's dark promises, of the deal he'd struck beneath this ground that hummed with the clang of picks and shovels.

The trees parted around the garish home of a noble mine owner. He dismounted behind the queen in their front cobbled courtyard as she swiftly dismounted and bid the lord good day and asked after satchels laden with taxes paid in blood opals from the gaunt and dower lord. The brief conversation that passed between them was nothing but a high-pitched hum in his ears as cold sweat trickled down the ridges of his spine. This place was too like the home of the overseer who'd kept him as his property for so long. Though this bastard's face wasn't one he recognized from his years spent as a slave, that didn't mean he hadn't bought valkry children off the Mad Queen for cheap labor in his own pits somewhere else.

The lord looked displeased, his waxy face and molted wings drooped and twisted, but he bowed his hunched back to his queen nonetheless as his servants tied the bounty to their nags. Oci squeezed his eyes shut, trying to get a grip on the bloody vengeance that stirred in his gut. It hissed and spit and demanded to be satiated, but that wouldn't do. He'd spent far too long plotting to waste it all now on one petty death.

The scuff of the queen's boots on stone as she turned snapped his eyes open. She nodded to him, and then they were remounting and leaving. The pressure in his skull eased with each hoofbeat that took them away from the black stone walls of the lord's keep.

"Give me a lie, Oci." The queen nudged her beast closer to his, so their thighs barely brushed against one another, startling him out of his dark reverie. He glanced up through the loose black strands of his hair that hung across his forehead to find her eyes searching his face, trying to read him but masking it with a playful curl to her lips.

He cleared his throat, though his words came out rasped and rubbed raw, "Aye, well, the woods are my favorite. I love the stinking scent of pine."

She laughed, though it sounded a bit dense, when her laugh yesterday was as light as a flock of songbirds taking flight. "Yes, well, I confess they aren't my favorite either."

He briefly thought to ask what it was that bothered her about the trees but thought better of it, it felt too close to true caring. "Time for your lie, Majesty, let's make it a good one."

There was a long silence filled only by the cursed wind in the damned trees, one that, thank Fates, no longer carried the ghosts of promises and blood oaths past. When Safiya finally spoke, her words were thick. "I got the scar on my lips from a riding accident."

He'd wondered, of course, how she'd gotten it, but he'd thought it ill-advised to ask, especially when she seemed so sensitive about it. He often caught her absentmindedly running a finger across it —too many times to count. "Well,"—he injected as much teasing into his words as he thought he could get away with to steer them away from talking about anything too intimate— "I did suspect you might secretly be clumsy."

She threw back her head and laughed, but then the melody cut off, cocooned in a strangled sound as it metamorphosed into a blood-chilling scream. Before Oci could scan the woods in search of whatever it was that had drawn such a reaction from her, her beast threw its hooves into the air, its whinnying cry sliced through the morning air, dousing him with surprise and something akin to fear.

The queen's scarlet hair loosed from whatever pins she had it in, sending it cascading down her back as she struggled to regain control of her frantic horse, but to no avail, the Fates damned creature took off down the trail in a fervent hoof-pounding gallop.

"Fates be fucked," Oci swore, and heeled his mount after her.

They broke from the path, splintering off into the dense wood, over ribbon-thin creeks and dense scrubbed underbrush, but Oci knew the area well. He split from her tail, angled his beast away, charging through the trees. He climbed from his stirrups, his fingers knotted in the beast's mane for stability, and raised himself into a crouch atop his saddle. With a shouted command at his horse to follow him, a demand all army nags were trained to learn, he launched himself, wings beating nearly as fast as his blood through his veins, into the air. He flew up and over his horse, pumping his wings as hard as he could to gain ground. He skimmed the outer edge of the forest, cutting as low as he could to catch a glimpse at where the queen's rogue creature careened headlong toward what he knew was a hidden maze of weak ground from a long-since abandoned web of mine tunnels. The tree branches above her caged her, preventing her from taking flight from the saddle as he had.

Oci's eyes ran rapidly across the woodland, assessing, waiting. The trees around the queen thinned ever so slightly, he just had to pick an opening and swoop in after her, pull her from her horse's back, and hope that the Fates would be merciful to them in their landing. It wasn't the trickiest bit of flying he'd ever done, but it always seemed to be the simplest shit that got grunts like him killed.

His eyes snagged on an opportunity, a small brown gap in the otherwise endless sea of green mere feet from where a chasm cut a bloody red stone swath through the trees. Sweat poured down his back, and his muscles screamed as he strained to overtake horse and rider. He was almost there. He had one chance to do this right, or he would lose her to the stony fall. That was not the death she was meant for. He dropped so he was barely a breath above the treetops, directly above them.

Oci broke over the gash in the trees at the exact moment the queen did; the Fates themselves couldn't have timed it better. He dropped, arms outstretched. He fisted the billowing purple skirts of her gown and yanked with all his might, popping her from her saddle like a tender bit of meat from a shellfish. He tucked her into his body, his arms snaking protectively around her thick waist, and cradled her head into the hollow of his shoulder as the force of his fall and the abruptness of his grab threw them both backward. He backpedaled with his wings in a vain effort to slow their fall. When the ground struck, the brunt of the blow slapped the air from him.

For a dizzying skull-splitting moment, Oci forgot how to breathe, then the sand sifted from his lungs, and he took his first ragged breath. A squirm across his chest reminded him he still had his arms locked around his queen. He let them slip down around her curvaceous waist to settle on the swell of her hips as she sat, straddling him, her face flushed nearly as scarlet as her hair, amber eyes wide and her breaths shallow. Inexplicably, heat sharply gutted him with the sudden and startling desire to see her again, just like this, but with much less between them.

He reached up and brushed her wind-swept hair from her cheek, tucking it over her shoulder as she braced her palms on his chest. "Are you all right, Oci?"

Her voice was drowning and choked with worry as she took his stubbled face in her hands, her fingers soothing as they brushed across his forehead and down his neck. He couldn't help it, he laughed. "You damn fool woman, your horse takes off with you nearly sending you over a cliff, and you're worried about me?"

Safiya smiled, her fangs brushing her lower lip. "You're the fool." She laughed incredulously, shoving off him before holding out a hand to help him to his feet, which he took, his large palms swallowing hers. "You came crashing through the damned trees. What if you'd punctured a wing?"

With a scowl, he brushed dirt from his leathers. "I'm no novice when it comes to tricky flight maneuvers. I'm a soldier, remember? Besides, I'm your bonded, aren't I? I couldn't very well let your fucking nag take you for a dive off the edge of the chasm ahead, could I?"

The fucking woman just shook her head and started stalking off through the trees in a snap of twigs and a flurry of skirts. "I had it well in hand."

Oci gawked after her. "Well in hand my ass."

"Are you coming or not? We must get moving if we're to find my horse and return to the caravan before nightfall. There isn't time to stand in the woods and admire the scenery," she called back to him.

"Right, because that's what I'm doing, admiring the bloody fucking scenery." He strode after her, stomping through the brush.

They called for her horse, and despite no evidence that it had plunged to its death, they also could find no evidence that it survived, leaving them with only one horse between them and little time to waste getting back.

"We can't both ride one poor horse," the queen argued. Women, they always needed to argue every damn point. "You can ride, and I'll fly." She offered the option as though it were the most rational and sane thought, when it obviously wasn't.

"No. What if there's a danger and you're too far ahead or above? Not going to happen." He shook his head, strands of hair slipped free from the leather he had it knotted up in.

"I'm perfectly capable of handling myself, but if you insist, you can fly, and I'll ride." She crossed her arms in that stubborn way of hers, as pouty and petulant as any barmaid right before she caved and let him take her to bed. She was tired, he could see it in the faint purple smudges under her eyes, and while he hadn't yet asked what it was that made her scream and spooked her horse, he had a sinking suspicion that it was the Honey hallucinations beginning to set in.

"Like I'd let you go haring off on my horse," he growled. "Besides, it can handle us both just fine, it's of an old valkry warhorse breed, paid a pretty bit for it too. Now get your royal ass on that nag or I'll put you on it."

Her eyes narrowed, and she pressed her full lips into an impossibly thin line. "You wouldn't dare. I'm your queen."

"And I'm your bloody bonded, now get on the horse." And then as though it were an afterthought, her added, "Your Majesty." He took a step forward, his hand held out, ready to grab her, his lips curled in a fang-tipped smile that silently said he knew she knew he'd won.

She made an indignant noise and a rude gesture that he returned with a smirk as soon as her back was turned. He should have let her fall into the gorge and break her fool neck for all the thanks he was getting. But he wasn't quite done with her yet. Besides, *they* wouldn't have liked that, *they* needed her alive, and he needed *them*.

He helped her mount, then swung up behind her. The pair of them rode on in stilted silence, squeezed into the large, though admittedly not large enough saddle that had the swell of her thick ass rolling unfortunately into his groin with every step. Oci tried to urge the beast faster, but that only seemed to make the situation worse. The queen's breaths came in short gasps, which he could feel in the heave and swell of her breasts against the arm he had wrapped securely around her. He could practically smell her arousal, though he thought he may have imagined it, the heady scent crafted in his mind by his own desire. The Fates had to be fucking with him.

As he fought away lusty imaginings, a dark and twisted voice echoed in the back of his mind. A voice he wasn't sure was his or theirs. Its smoky and thorned words reminded him of the plan, that prey was much easier to slaughter if you could make it love you first. But he argued back, with them or with himself—what happened if the predator fell for his prey?

Chapter 36

Safiya and Ocidynus arrived at camp just as the sky shed its sunny blue day dress in exchange for a sultry purple nightgown studded with pearly stars.

Safiya dismounted with a word to the sentries that met them like panicked bees buzzing about a hive to take the blood opals to the treasurer for safekeeping and commanded that a bath be sent to her tent as soon as possible. She needed to wash the smell of him from her skin. It was intoxicating, and she couldn't think clearly with it clinging to her like a sheer veil.

Her bonded's steps echoed hers across the packed sand. Though as if he could sense her need for space, her need to breathe air that wasn't saturated by him, he stopped outside the canvas tent flaps. She tore her riding clothes from her body, cutting straight through the laces with an elongated talon, and shed them on the floor like a snake molting from its skin. But even naked, there was still too much of him wrapped around her for comfort. The smell was hedonistic, heady, making her insides writhe, making them throb. She was too hot all over, and yet her body ached for the searing sensation of him pressed against her.

She could feel his touch like a phantom, his arm wrapped around her middle. She stalked to the trunk next to the fireplace where a decanter of bloodred wine and two crystal goblets sat. She poured herself a drink, her hands trembling with sharp need or withdrawals she wasn't sure. The red drink spilled over, sloshing onto the carpeted tent floor as she took it in hand and brought it to her lips and let its chilled and bitter taste ground her. Her breaths evened as she set the drained glass back in its place.

The shimmer of her bathing robe from where it hung off the back of her chair by the fire caught her gaze. She poured another glass before crossing the cramped tent space and wrapping herself in the soft near-sheer fabric. Safiya absently swirled the wine in her cup. She tried not to look at the vacant chair that sat opposite the small table before her, set with a stones board. It gave her all sorts of notions that she couldn't quite rationalize, but in not looking at it, her gaze snagged instead on the silhouetted form of her bonded, her poisoner, the source of the fire that rushed through her veins. "Oci, come in here, please."

His shoulders tensed before he slowly turned, pulled aside the tent flap, and ducked in. He went to one knee before her in an overly formal gesture, but when his golden eyes met hers, there was mischief in them. A little thrill shot through her like a falling star, before crashing into her core where it burned brightly. "How can I be of service, my Queen?"

Oh, she ran a fang over her lip, she could think of so many ways. "Didn't we agree to call one another by our names?" she sighed, "Play a game of stones with me while I wait for my bath."

He quirked an eyebrow, and the hint of a smile played across his sensual mouth. "As you wish." He stood, his eyes locked on hers as he slowly undid his sword belt and slung it over the chair before he sat. "I believe your color plays first, Safiya." Her name rolled off his tongue as if he liked the taste of it in his mouth.

She suppressed a shiver as she leaned forward and plucked up a white stone, smooth and cool in her fingers, and placed it. She leaned back, satisfied with her opening move, but Oci tsked, his eyes boring into hers mercilessly. "Wrong move."

Safiya crossed and recrossed her legs as she watched Oci's scarred hands deftly shift pieces counter to hers, each movement somehow stoking the incandescently bright inferno within her. When his turn was finished, he took her wine chalice and stood to refill it for her and pour himself a glass before returning to their game.

His eyes were on her like a brand, burning a path as his gaze traced her cheekbones, down the point of her chin, the long column of her neck, before they dipped to the slight opening of her robe below the hollow of her throat. She took a sip, Honey sweet, as it always was when he served her. A thought struck her, and the sour taste of remorse overtook the poisonously saccharine flavor that lingered. She leaned in to make her move, and asked, "You seemed rather familiar with this area today, Oci. Tell me, were you here as a child?"

His shoulders stiffened as they had on the hill that morning, and she found hers doing the same, mirroring his response or bracing for his words. This had to be it. The reason the Fates had chosen him as her executioner. Was it perhaps not because she'd killed her mother that they sought retribution, mayhap her true crime had not been intervening earlier? But she too had been a child when the war broke out, and her mother held her secrets tightly in her clawed fist. But then again, who was she to argue with the Fates or try to rationalize their decisions? Safiya let her gaze flick to Oci's face; his expression was one carved carefully of cold neutrality. Breath caught against her ribs as she waited for his reply.

"I am well acquainted with the mines near here if that's what you're asking." His words were hollowed out.

She traced her scar across her lips as she often did when thinking of her mother. "I'm sorry for what she did to your people."

His gaze collided with hers, something wicked sparked to life in their depths. "As apologies go, that's a bit pitiful, don't you think?" He leaned back in his chair, the picture of indolence, his chin resting on his fist. So this was to be another game, then. She understood as she saw the smoldering behind his golden eyes that he was toying with her as if he were a Tatzelwurm and she his supper.

"And what do you think would make it more sincere?" She leaned forward and shifted a single stone along the board.

He immediately took it with one of his as she suspected he might. "Kneel." The single word purred across the space between them.

Safiya arched a crimson brow. "I'm the queen. I kneel before no one."

He leaned back, that arrogant tilt to his head again, his lips curled into a predatory smile. "You'll kneel before me."

The queen's heart throbbed against her ribs, and as though tethered together by a string, so too did that brilliant burning in her core. Her whole body ached with a curiosity pulled so taut it bordered on need. The singular question surged through her veins with every thwomp of her heart. What would he do if she did as he asked?

Oci's pupils blew wide as she rose, smooth as silk. His teeth clenched as though to stop his jaw from going slack as she gracefully went to her knees before him, the slit of her robe parting to expose the swell of her rich bronze thigh.

The queen's hands pressed into his leather-clad knees, and she bent her head and let her hair spill across his lap. "I am truly sorry for what my mother did all those years ago." And she was from the depths of her being truly full of remorse. She would forever carry the stain of being the daughter of the Mad Queen, haunted by the past that she could not undo. Tentatively, she peered up to look into his face so he could see the sincerity that poured from her heart.

The fire in the hearth crackled as her bonded's eyes slowly perused her face before he shifted, leaning in to grip her chin between his thumb and forefinger. The pad of his thumb brushed over the bottom of the scar on her lips, and she shuddered as he rasped, "Never apologize for that bitch again, Safiya."

Her breath swept from her lungs in a rush, and the next thing she knew, she was in his lap, unsure if she'd climbed into it or if he'd hoisted her up or if they were drawn together, pulled as inevitably as the moon pulled the tides. And then their lips collided, and it no longer mattered who'd moved first. All that mattered was their tangled bodies and the overwhelmingly dark and sweet taste of him.

His hands wrapped around her waist, drawing her in, pressing her against the firm planes of his body, their hips rolling into one another, his evident arousal ground against the apex of her thighs as he devoured her soft moans of pleasure. Was this what it was to grow in love for another as an equal, she wondered as he thrust against her, his mouth leaving hers to lick up the column of her throat as she panted his name, her fingers tangled in the black locks of his hair.

The calluses of his sword-hardened hands scraped against the outside of her thighs before deftly slipping beneath the hem of her robe and around her hips where they kneaded her backside, grinding her harder against the length of him. Oci nipped her ear. "Tell me, my Queen, how long —"

His words were cut off with a groan as she worked her hand into the open laces of his shirt—

The sound of hoof beats pounding against the dirt and echoed shouts outside had them springing apart so swiftly it left her breathless. By the time a messenger burst into her tent, she sat poised, if a little flushed and flustered, her robe neatly back in place with her glass of wine in hand as an excuse for her coloring. Oci stood, his hand resting on the back of his chair, looking so casual one would have never guessed a moment before that he'd been toying with her in his lap like a courtesan.

The messenger went to his knee before her, his wings tucked tightly at his back. "Forgive the intrusion at such a late hour, Majesty, but there have been creatures spotted in the nearby wood. One of the night watchmen also reported that he had his horse mauled by some beast, but he didn't get a good look at it. General Haken sent me immediately, he thought you would want to know first."

Safiya nodded, the lust and the wine haze bled out of her in an instant, leaving behind only the Honey residue to slow her thoughts, though not enough that she didn't recall Yarressa's words from the oasis. Out of the corner of her eye, she thought she saw her bonded pale, most likely concerned over this new potential threat to her safety. "Thank you for coming to me, Haken was correct. Has he organized a hunting party to track the creature?"

The messenger nodded. "He has, Your Majesty, and doubled the guard around camp."

"Good, please keep me apprised of any new information." She dismissed him with a wave of her hand. She turned to Oci, tempted to confide in him what the old tribeswoman had told her to garner his opinion, but the moment the flaps ceased to stir from the messenger's departure, they parted again to reveal a cluster of servants carting a small copper tub and buckets of steaming water. How could she have forgotten the Fates cursed bath that she'd ordered to scrub him off her. Now all she craved was the opposite.

Her attendants busied themselves setting everything up, and she couldn't very well dismiss them now after all the work they'd put in to bringing her such a luxury while surely having other things to tend to. Though she sorely wished she could.

Oci took his sword belt from the back of the chair and turned to duck out of the tent, but his name fell from her lips, freezing him in his tracks. He turned to look back at her over his shoulder, his voice thick as he answered the unasked question he must have gleaned from her gaze. "We will finish our game later, Safiya."

Though as she stepped into her bath, Safiya was suddenly unsure of which game he was referring to.

Chapter 37

Xandrina launched from her saddle into the sky as soon as the first shimmering ribbon of turquoise ocean appeared on the horizon. Salt teased through the air on the thick wet breeze that wreathed around her as she spiraled upward. The sound of wings beating below in echo to her own signaled that her bonded trailed in her wake. She surged ahead, silently teasing him into giving chase through the billowing clouds.

He finally caught up to her, his shadow wrapping around her from above. She rolled in the air, flipping upside down to face him. "Took you long enough, bonded." Her lips hitched into a smirking smile.

He rolled his peculiar eyes, though she thought she saw a hint of amusement, perhaps even happiness in them, as his hair came unbound from its knot and their wing tips brushed with every synchronous beat, perfect mirror opposites to one another.

"We should go back." He nodded toward the fast-approaching blanket of blue sea just over the plunging lip of a cliff dotted with gaudy structures along its edge like over frosted tea cakes perched on a platter. "The queen will be furious if you aren't there when they ride through the gates."

It was her turn to roll her eyes. "Don't you think it's ridiculous to ride when we can fly?"

He shrugged infuriatingly and without waiting dove past her, brushing her cheek with a black feather tip as he plunged toward the twisting column of the caravan spread serpentine across the red sands that gave way to packed ground and long rush-like grasses.

With a snarled sigh, she followed, rolling and angling her wings back, surging through the air to gain on him, their silent competition continued. She grinned, self-satisfaction purring through her belly as she landed atop her nickering horse a breath before he landed atop his, only jostling Lyrahvi in her basket ever so slightly with her touchdown. She threw a smugly victorious look at him over her shoulder to which he shook his head in a way that might have been called annoyed had it been on anyone else, but she thought it indulgent.

Flirting with Snack again I see, Lyra purred.

I'm not flirting, I'm competing, trying to get under his skin as it were. Though she had to admit she wasn't ready yet to give up the easy and casual nature that she and Abrax had found together on the road and exchange it for the pomp and double-edged nature that came with noble functions.

Lyra narrowed her feline eyes, her gaze flicking between the two of them. *I see no difference.* She nestled back down into her basket and began grooming herself, licking her paws and her tail. *Besides, if you want to know what he's really thinking, you could just dredge up his emotions from the back of your head, Pet. You don't have to go through all the trouble of . . . competing.*

Lyra's last word licked around her mind with a condescending curl to it. *That's too intimate.*

And getting under his skin is not? The Tatzelwurm chortled when Xandrina declined responding, choosing instead to sneak a glance at her bonded, only to find his eyes already on her. She tried to stem the crimson tide of embarrassment that began to swell across her cheeks by quickly adverting her eyes, though she knew she'd failed when Lyra began giggling at her expense, the sound of it echoed mercilessly around her head.

The horses a pace ahead of hers—her mother's and that of her bonded—slowed as they approached a corral gate tangled in vines with tightly closed and twisted buds littered in the leaves, the entry to a winding road up a rise crowned at its pinnacle with a grand estate. A small entourage was assembled beneath the arch astride horses, which seemed more than a bit pretentious to her considering the estate was a mere minutes' flight if that.

Xandrina skimmed the faces of those who waited atop the stamping and huffing steads to greet them, each as forgettable as the last, though she imagined they had to be of some import to warrant a royal visit. Her perusal snagged on one that stuck out, slightly more familiar than the rest, with a smarmy smile and a wink that seemed to be reserved just for her. The unwanted attention made her insides feel like shriveling up. It was the bespectacled dullard from the very first ball the night of her crowning, the one whose name had slipped from her mind the moment he'd uttered it, though something about shipping lanes caught like a barb in her memory.

Well, well, I don't think Snack cares for the way that one is looking at you, Pet, Lyra purred in a mockingly singsong voice, but Xandrina refused to give her the satisfaction of looking over her shoulder at her bonded, again. She knew the look he likely had on his face well.

She watched the noble family bow at the waist as best as they could from horseback, their wings tucked awkwardly as they offered promises of baths, feasting, and festivities followed by talks of trade. Xandrina silently preened; she'd been right about the boring noble son, his family must guard the shipping lanes, which meant it was important for her to have him on her side especially with the seemingly endless unrest between her people and the harpies of the outlying island nations. How unfortunate. She waited until the nobleman's son was looking at her again, then she winked, a slight curl to her lips that showed just a hint of her fangs. He puffed his chest like an overconfident rooster. Well, at least it seemed he was easy to please.

I wouldn't be so sure about that, Pet, Lyra mused in answer to her thoughts. *Be careful, I don't like the look of him. Sometimes the vilest of creatures make themselves look bland so they can bite when you least expect.*

Xandrina heeled herself forward as their party began to follow their hosts up the hill. *I guess my bite will just have to be sharper.*

Chapter 38

Oci tried not to watch the seductive sway to Safiya's hips and instead tried to take better note of their surroundings as he followed a half step behind her through the breezy halls of the quaint seaside palace as a blathering maid led them to the royal guest suite. It was garishly lavish with a spacious sitting room that had adjoining doors that branched off into twin bedrooms. It's high arching windows spilled out onto a broad sweeping balcony overlooking the vast expanse of open water dotted with clusters of billowing sails and spits of infantile isles. Oci blinked, and for a heartbeat, he saw the waters bleed red, the waves heaving buoyant bodies of the fallen instead of skiffs and gulls. By the next beat, it returned to its normal turquoise.

"Are you listening to me, Oci?" Safiya's tone was clipped with enough worry that he unconsciously fisted the hilt of his sword, ready for any perils.

He relaxed his grip when he found her seated on a low settee with no pressing danger other than perhaps a paper cut from the parchment she held. Well, and him. "Apologies, my Queen, what is it you were saying?"

She sighed, sweeping her hair over her shoulder, drawing his eyes unconsciously to the place he'd pressed his lips the night before. "This missive, it's from Idris. There is some concern over Cato, it seems he's not returned, which is decidedly odd. He did say that he was going straight back, did he not?"

Oci grunted noncommittally, he didn't care much for the Travelers and their problems, not like the beasts he worked with, not like the voices. He had room in his head for only one revenge plot, and that was becoming convoluted as it was with lust. The queen crossed her legs, drawing the fabric of her riding pants taut against the swell of her ample hips. Fates fuck him, why couldn't she have been a shriveled hag?

She tossed the letter down beside her and met his gaze with eyes shot through with the red of exhaustion and the faintest yellowy tinge of the illness brought on by her excessive Honey consumption. "I didn't mention it before, but it feels prudent to now, the beast the soldier saw, it's not the first report of them I've had."

Swearing internally, Oci gritted his teeth, he could feel the beasts she spoke of circling, keeping just enough distance to prevent detection but close enough to come if he summoned them. He was meant to be their master for the time being, but he felt the reins he had on them slipping just enough. They were getting restless. Their master, and his too he supposed, wanted the queen. They wanted him done with her, and he was close, so close to getting what he desired, what he needed, and then he could give her up. But could he? A small voice in the back of his head whispered, could he really hand her over to whatever fate would await her at the hands of those monstrosities?

The queen chewed her lower lip, deep in thought. "I can't help feeling the two are connected somehow, Cato's delayed return and the creatures, if only I could find the threads to tie the incidences together."

"I don't see how the two could be related," Oci said smoothly, belaying none of his concerns, but he'd gone preternaturally still, his hand on the hilt of his sword. Perhaps she was right, the voices after all had asked for the strongest Travelers. They didn't divulge the full extent of their plans. It wasn't a stretch to think they were hunting those with great strength outside of this little fractured slice of existence. But what the fuck did it matter if they were? It wasn't for him to question their schemes outside of his part in them. He loosed the grip on his hilt and stuffed his hands into his pocket. He felt the vial lying within, and a cold fist slipped around his heart, no. Now was not the time for questions and faltering.

Safiya crumpled the paper in her fist, her talons shredding into it, ripping it to ribbons with half a thought and a frustrated sound. "I don't know. I suppose I'm just grasping at frayed ends trying to braid a rug." She kicked off her slippers and leaned back against the settee, tucking her feet up under her in a sprawl of feminine sighs. She pressed her fingers to her temples and began to massage them in slow circles. "Some days I'm just so very tired, Oci."

He moved to stand behind her, slipping his fingers in place of hers rubbing her distress away, luxuriating in the feel of her hair running like strands of spider silk between his fingers and loathing himself for it. She tipped her head back further, relaxing it into the cradle of his hands, trusting him so completely.

"Let me carry the burden for you, Safiya." His rasped and raw words stilled her breaths. Her eyes fluttered open, and they were so fucking full of adoration. He should have been pleased, his plan to seduce her was working. Of course it was, he'd seduced many women, so why then did the hollow within his ribcage ache with such a vacuous intensity that it felt like it should be snapping bones?

Without examining the urge too closely lest he find fault in it, he leaned forward, cupped a hand under his queen's chin and tilted her lips up to meet his in a bruising and punishing kiss. Fire replaced the ache in his bones, burning and consuming it and reshaping him at his core, filling him with a want and a lust so savage it became a groaning beast of its own.

Safiya whimpered deliciously beneath him, and the beast within went feral, deepening the kiss until it was all tongues, nipping teeth, and wonton need. The creek of door hinges sent them flying apart and left him uncomfortably aching in his leathers as a full retinue of servants poured in lugging trunks and cases from the caravan to be settled in their rooms.

His queen hurriedly addressed the servants, directing them where to go and with what, while he quickly and discreetly sneaked out onto the balcony overlooking the sea to give himself a bloody moment to compose himself. He slipped a hand into his pocket and pulled forth the stoppered vial. He would have to replenish his supply, otherwise that woman would be the death of him.

Chapter 39

The music from the night's festivities raced along the sultry sea breeze and into the windows of the princess's suite. A maid provided by the residing noble family busied herself with Xandrina's hair, using a hot iron to tease it into a spill of copper coils before pinning it with golden pins tipped with carved bees.

When she was finished, the maid bowed and slipped back toward a full-length mirror in the corner, silently requesting that the princess come and approve her outfit. Xandrina obliged, standing and sweeping her way across the teal sea glass–tiled floors. Her full tulle skirt tulipped in cerulean waves from just above her navel down to the floor, every inch of it embroidered in swirling, shimmering golden thread and beading. The corset she wore was cropped just above the groove of her ribcage, leaving a significant strip of her skin bare. The near-sheer fabric would have left her entirely exposed were it not for clever and elegant beadwork stitched in cascading turquoise, pearl, and gold. She had to admit that the effect was pleasing, making her look like the sea at sunset when the tired sun wept the last of its gilded rays into the water. The serving girl had even gone so far as to dust her wings with gleaming aureate powders so no matter which way she turned she caught the light.

Xandrina curtly nodded her approval and her dismissal to the woman who stood hands clasped and waiting. Her brow furrowed when the women faltered, seeming to stall, her lips working as though she chewed on unsaid words. Xandrina sighed and gave the woman her best smile, which annoyingly only seemed to make the woman pale. "Is there something you wish to say?"

The woman gnawed at her lip, her downcast eyes darting and skipping across the tiles at her feet. The princess sighed and was about to speak again when the woman's words suddenly spewed out in a tumbled half-mad rush. "It's the lordling, highness, you'd do well to stay away from him. He has a reputation is all, and I wouldn't want for him to . . ." She stalled again, but this time it was with a whimper of obvious fear that the words froze on her lips.

Lyrahvi slithered up onto the bed behind them, and in the mirror's reflection, Xandrina could see her ears perked and listening. *This one is afraid for her life, the stench of it is all over the room*, the Tatzelwurm hissed suspiciously across her mind.

"Wouldn't want for him to what?" Xandrina stepped closer, smoothly setting a hand on the quavering woman's shoulder in what she hoped was a reassuring way. She let a small trickle of magic leak from her fingers, just a little spell laced with calm. "It's all right, you're safe here. I will neither report you for what you say nor reprimand you. You can speak your piece."

The woman relaxed so visibly it made Xandrina wonder at what kind of people her employers were. "He, well, he likes to coerce women, with the Honey. It's no ordinary honey, Highness, it does things. It muddies the mind, makes colors brighter and sounds sweeter, it makes you do things you wouldn't normally do, Highness. People take a little for fun, you see, but he always makes certain to give his, company, too much."

The princess frowned, beginning to see the shape of the picture the woman was painting. "Let me guess, you wake with a head full of regret and a broken heart with no recourse to punish him seeing as you technically agreed to whatever it was the lordling suggested?" Her words were spat full of venom.

Tears welled in the maid's eyes, and she nodded through a choked sob. "Yes, highness, that is the sum of it."

"And how many has he done this to?" Xandrina fought to keep the seething hatred she felt from creeping into her voice, to keep her talons from lengthening, ready to rip out throats.

The woman's breaths were nearing hysterical. "I don't know any who he hasn't done it to, Princess."

Her tears then fell in earnest, her small body crumpling in on itself like a wilting flower. It was then that Xandrina noticed the slight swell of her belly, and she truly understood the severity of the situation. The bastard had impregnated her. Xandrina pulled the woman into a fierce hug, smoothing back her hair and humming calming placations until the woman's cries metamorphosed into hiccups and her wings sagged off her back.

"Tell me your name," Xandrina demanded gently as she guided the maid to sit on the edge of her bed, her wing curled around the woman protectively.

"Umbri," she answered through sniffles, her brown eyes scored through with threads of crimson sorrows.

"I have a proposition for you, Umbri. How would you like to become one of my personal lady's maids? You can come back to the capital with me, have your babe in peace. If you wish to give it up, I will find it a loving noble family who will raise it as their own, and if you wish to keep it, I will give you a lifelong position that will afford you the best of child care and enough money to send him or her to a good school when they come of age along with a trust in their name and a pension for you to retire on."

I would have offered her the man's sack on a string to wear as a necklace, but that seems like a generous enough offer, Lyrahvi snarled as she curled up next to Umbri and rested her head in her lap.

That's disgusting. Though Xandrina had to admit it would be poetic in a gruesome sort of way.

"I can't possibly, an urchin like me has no—" Umbri tried to protest.

"Enough of that." Xandrina placed a claw delicately across her lips to silence her. "I will hear no self-deprecations. If you wish to decline my offer because you have family here or for another legitimate reason, that's acceptable. I will still make sure you and your babe are well cared for and not working here. What I will not stand for is your rejection because you think you aren't worthy; he is the one who is not worthy, Umbri."

Snack is waiting for you. He's pacing again. Lyra flicked her gaze toward the door.

Xandrina folded Umbri into one last embrace. "I have to go, find me before we leave with your answer."

Umbri nodded with utterances of thanks as she stood and disappeared through the narrow servant's entrance behind a faded tapestry of a long-ago sea battle.

Before heading out the door, Xandrina paused at her weapons chest at the foot of her bed and retrieved a couple of spare knives, which she sheathed discreetly wherever her scant clothing would allow.

What are you planning, Pet? You know you can't kill the bastard without serious political ramifications, as much as you and I would both enjoy that. Lyra rolled over onto her back, batting at a tassel hanging from the bedcurtain's ties, pretending, no doubt, that it was the lordling's face.

Don't worry, Lyra, I'm not going to kill him. I just want to play with him. The corners of her lips curled in a vicious smirk as she slipped out of her room to the sound of Lyra's yowling approval.

Chapter 40

Safiya leaned against the arched balcony threshold, her wings curled in around slumped shoulders. Sweat beaded her brow, threatening to ruin the cosmetics painted carefully on her face. Nausea rolled in her stomach in time with the lurch and crash of the waves below. She was not ready for this night, for this death. She wanted to scream at the skies and beg the Fates to change their minds. She wanted to understand, but all she understood was that she had to do this to save her daughter. But as she watched clouds crowd the horizon, a tugging sense of unease made her question if the throne was the safest place for her daughter to be. After all, no queen of Gypette had lived a long life.

"Majesty," a murmur drew Safiya's attention to where Marryn crept like a spider from the shadows of her room, "I have"—the woman swallowed hard—"I have something for you, a tidbit I picked up accidentally while in the library this afternoon."

The queen straightened, drawing herself up to her full regal height despite the dizzying protests of her mind and body. "Out with it, please, I'm due downstairs."

The woman wrung her hands around a jagged-edged piece of paper before handing it over. "I don't know if it is what I think it is. It's probably nothing, I ought not to have bothered you with it I'm sure—" She trailed off, but Safiya could feel the intensity of her eyes watching her as she unfolded the scrap of parchment.

It was a lineage, obviously torn from a book, the last line of the valkry royals to be more specific. Her eyes traced the branches of the family tree, scanning and missing what it was Marryn was so concerned with when a name written in tight looping script at the bottom hooked her attention. She snapped the paper in half concealing its contents.

"Well, thank you for bringing this to me, but like you said Marryn, this is probably nothing. A simple coincidence, I'm sure."

Her servant and spy curtsied. "As you say, my Queen. I apologize for disturbing you."

Safiya unfurled the page and once more ran her gaze over the final line. "*Prince Erron Ocidynus Althorn, black of hair and golden of eye, born under the Fates moon of Fortune in the year 1641.*" The words felt like a curse and a blessing, as understanding often does.

It felt as though all the Fates' eyes were upon her as she shredded the parchment, tossed it into the night's breeze, and watched as the wind pulled it out to the ocean.

Chapter 41

Abrax watched as the princess spilled into the room like sunlight lighting up the party with her luminescent presence. Heads gravitated toward her like flowers starved for her warmth and attention, as in awe of her power and beauty as he was.

He'd entered just ahead of her and done a quick sweep around the room. As always, he would keep on the periphery, orbiting her, surveying for any threats. The lordling, Ivar, strutted to her almost instantly, a smarmy smile painted on his distinctly plain face, his feathers ruffled cockily. Abrax recalled him from his first night in the palace; he'd been dancing with the princess on the veranda. The memory tasted sour in the back of his throat.

The taste of it only deepened as Ivar took Xandrina's hand, bent low over it, and pressed a kiss to her coppery skin, his lips lingering just a fraction longer than Abrax felt was truly necessary. He licked his lips with a disgusting wink as he rose, and Fates be fucked . . . Xandrina batted her eyelashes at him. She never batted her eyelashes. Ever. What, he wondered, could she possibly be playing at? His family seat was important but not that important.

Ivar bent to whisper in her ear, Abrax's hands clenched with the unconscious desire to strangle and maim, but Xandrina giggled and nodded, agreeing to a dance. Abrax waited, his pulse throbbed beneath his skin in a torrent as he watched Xandrina gaze at the lordling adoringly, not snapping once as his hand slipped boldly lower and lower as he danced them toward a shadowy balcony exit.

Abrax followed, keeping to the periphery, mere heartbeats behind them. For her safety, he reminded himself as heat crept up the back of his neck, not so he could twist the sphynx's neck and rip his head from his body. A drunken group of revelers cut off his view of the princess as they crashed from an alcove in a riot of too loud laughter and smeared makeup onto the dance floor. His breaths came rapidly, sawing in and out of him in a desperate attempt to keep his composure as he tripped around a table heading for the door. He needed to have eyes on her. It could take only moments for a man to harm her, to compromise her. To kiss her.

He rounded the exit, his ears perked for any sound. There. The whispered thread of conversation just barely audible as it slipped between the ever-present beat of the sea and the rabble of the party. He grasped onto it and tugged, reeling himself toward the faint lilting and hissed voice that he knew better than he knew his own. It drew him along the sumptuous curves of the garden filled with secluded spaces for lovers and low-growing shrubby flowers that flung themselves across the ground toward the cliff's edge that lay mere feet from the keep.

Tucked against the coral stone wall under an awning of twining vines covered in flowers, twisted shut tight as though they wished to keep secrets, he found them, and his heart stopped so swiftly it ricochet off his ribs and slammed into his spine. Ivar had Xandrina pressed against the shadowed wall, his head dipped against her neck, his hand gripping a coppery swell of thigh beneath bunched-up layers of skirt.

Abrax was about to make his presence known, violently, when Xandrina's gaze cut swiftly to his, a coppery blade in the dark. She gave him an ever so subtle shake of her head. It was then that he noticed the way her hand fisted the lordling's golden curls, her claws extended and gleaming with her cosmic luminescent magic. A slow drip of blood seeped down the back of Ivar's neck, staining the collar of his dusk-blue shirt just visible between the swell of his tightly held wings.

He nodded his understanding, and his heart rate slowed. Whatever was going on, it was going precisely as she wanted it to, and he took a step back to hide in the shadowy recesses beside the trellis. As he moved, he caught the silvery hint of moonlight glinting off a dagger pressed against the lordling's groin, and he grinned. Fates fuck him, but she was devastatingly beautiful when she had a knife to another man's crotch, or maybe he was just fucked in the head. Either way, it was not an image he would soon forget.

Abrax pressed himself to the wall next to her with only the curtain of foliage between them. He tipped his head closer, the curled blooms brushed against his cheek, to listen to her whispered words. "Don't worry, Lordling"—she spat the title so venomously Ivar hissed as if bitten—"my magic will hold you to your vow for the rest of your days. If you so much as think of touching another soul without their consent, if you so much as go near the Honey with the intent of using it unwittingly on another, your blood will boil, and your little bitty cock will shrivel into dust. Understood?"

Abrax fisted the hilt of his sword; the bastard was a rapist. His lips curled, and it was an effort to still himself against the coral wall and silently let the princess dole out justice as she saw fit when every instinct in him screamed to rip through the vines separating them and tear out his throat and toss him off the cliff to be food for the long-toothed carnivorous eels that sometimes frequented these shores.

Ivar growled, "You bitch."

Xandrina tsked at him as if he were no more than a naughty pet. "Now, now, that's not nice."

The lordling muttered indecipherably, followed by a sharp intake of breath threaded with toothy notes of panic. "Oops," the princess said blandly, "my knife slipped just a bit. I didn't quite here what you said . . ."

"All right, all right!" Ivar panted pitifully. "I understand, I understand, now please let me go, please. I'll behave, by the Fates I swear it!"

"Oh, and one more thing, Ivar," Xandrina purred as Ivar sniffled and whimpered damply, "you'll tell no one about this, and you'll support my mother and I implicitly in all our council decisions regarding the shipping lanes, trade, and anything else we might need backed by your family. You're our most loyal supporter, are you not?"

There was another despicably weak squeak. "Yes, yes of course, highness, anything you need."

"And you'll do right by any bastards you've sired, funds for their mothers and educations, no need to interact with them directly, though, we wouldn't want your influence anywhere near impressionable young minds."

"Yes, okay fine, please," the pitiful excuse for a sphynx sobbed, "just please let me go."

There was a soft thud of a body hitting dirt followed by a scuffle of boots. Scrambling and hunched, Ivar bolted from the concealed nook back toward where light spilled across the lawn.

Xandrina spun around the edge of the trellis, a wicked smile playfully dancing on her lips that was all vengeance and glinting fangs. "Bastard pissed himself." She half laughed, gazing of in the direction the lordling ran. "Son of a bitch is lucky I let him keep his cock."

"I wouldn't have," Abrax admitted darkly from where he still leaned against the wall, his arms crossed across his broad chest to keep himself from rushing to her, from touching her to make sure she was all right.

The princess flicked her eyes to his, searching, her copper gaze predatory in the dark. "You overheard then?"

He shrugged, his black feathers rustling softly with the movement. "Some."

She sighed and withdrew a glass vial from where she had it tucked in her corseted top between her breasts. It was filled with deep amber liquid. "He was using Honey to lower women's inhibitions, then taking advantage. Apparently, it's a heck of a high if you take it for fun."

He kept his expression impassive, not wanting to let any of the loathing he felt for the lordling or concern he felt for her slip onto his face as he looked at the Honey, warm from being so close to her skin, coat the glass of the vial as she rolled it between her fingers. "I've heard."

Xandrina cocked her head questioningly, and he answered without her having to speak her thoughts aloud. "I was stationed at the nearby fort for a time, a few summers back when the harpie raiders were particularly active." For the briefest of moments, she glanced at the scars that marred the side of his face and neck, intuitively guessing that his time here was the reason he'd been maimed, but he was neither ready to confirm nor deny that for her, the trauma, though healed well on the surface, still festered in his heart. "Some of the men liked to take it while they were on leave." He could still recall how the cliffs not far from here wept the golden liquid from the hives built on its craggy face. The bees that produced it fed only from the poisonous flowers that wended next to him, and across every building in the region, the toxins from the flowers while perfectly harmless for the bees made their Honey hallucinogenic in small doses and deadly in larger ones or with prolonged use. He'd seen sphynx warriors brought to their knees with withdraws when the intoxicating effects wore off after days of endless usage, and some didn't recover at all.

"But you never . . ." She arched an amused eyebrow and inched closer to him.

He let his arms fall to his sides. "No, never."

"Want to try?" Her lips curled mischievously, and she flicked the stopper from the bottle's top as she closed the distance between them in a single step.

Xandrina was in his air, filling it with her cloying scent that wrapped around him like intoxicating beckoning fingers. "It would be irresponsible of me," he whispered, his breath stirring the loose strands of her hair that brushed her forehead.

She hooked her fingers over the collar of his leather jacket and pulled herself against him. She pressed her sultry lips to the mouth of the vial, and his eyes watched the long column of her throat as she tipped her head back and took the tiniest of sips, before offering it up to him. Her eyes watched him hungrily through her thick lashes. "Come on, Abrax, do something irresponsible for once. Let go with me."

Maybe it was the way she looked at him in that moment, or maybe it was the way she said those last words, but he wrapped his long and calloused fingers around her hand that fisted the vial and brought it to his lips and drank a few drops of the too sweet thick liquid, their locked gazes never wavering from each other.

A shudder ran through her as he let her hand fall. She cast the bottle onto the grass and laced her fingers tightly with his. She pulled him along behind her toward the cliff's edge, and together they took the plunge off the precipice.

Chapter 42

Safiya's head reeled as she accepted dance after dance from nobles and dignitaries alike. Her wine was laced, too sweet with the Honey she knew was slowly worming its way through her body. She could feel her bonded's eyes on her, searing all the points where she was being touched by another.

She wished it was him pulling her around the dance floor, his hands steady on her waist, grounding her when she felt as though she were coming undone. Little pieces of her tugged like ribbons unspooling in all directions.

Her steps faltered as she caught a glimpse over the shoulder of her dance partner of rotted lace and frayed flesh, of hollow eyes and an accusatory finger pointed at her, naming her, calling her out. The corpse of her mother strode across the ballroom floor with vengeance in her step, her face twisted in a silent scream. Decomposing minibeasts gnawed their way through her graying flesh. As she walked, the remnants of her wings screeched across the floor, little more than bone and sinew.

No one screamed, no one so much as twitched an eyelash, and the phantasmagorical sight of the Mad Queen. Not real then, a Honeyed hallucination. Safiya choked on a smothered laugh. Who was she to call her mother mad when it was now she that saw that which was not there? Unless she was there, sent from beyond the Veil to drag her daughter before the Fates of Death and Judgment to weigh her soul and her actions and find her wanting.

"Your majesty?" The words held a polite question, and she realized that she'd not only faltered but stilled, her hand caught on her throat.

She shoved a smile onto her face that felt too tight around the edges, too much fang in it, but there was no taking it back now. "I apologize, I think I'm a bit tired, long journey and all that. Thank you for the lovely dance."

Her dance partner started to speak— at the same moment his face began dripping like candle wax, catching and drawing his speech out, molding it into unrecognizable shapes. She gritted her teeth, pinning her smile on her cheeks, holding it there as if it could shield her from the world as she swept from the room. Each step away from the ballroom pressed on her, weighing and cinching. Her feet quickened, kicking off her slippers, her wings splayed out behind her. She ran as if she could somehow outrun her fate.

Safiya's breaths stuck, her lungs sucking against her ribs that stabbed like jagged glass shards. The floor bucked and rolled beneath her, the edges of her vision bruised. She crashed through the doors to her suite, leaving them gaping in her wake as the cool marble floor rose up to meet her, to caress her damp cheek. She tried in vain to draw in more air, but it came thickly in sips and slow trickles when she needed gulps of it.

Calloused hands grasped her shoulders and turned her over. Cold steel bit between her breasts, followed by ripping and shredding as Oci sliced through her corset like cake. He pulled her into his lap, cradling her, and pressed his forehead to hers, holding her there with fingers tangled in her hair. "Breathe, Saf, just breathe with me, in and out."

She patterned her breaths to his, willing her lungs to unstick, to inflate. Without the corset strangling her like death's fist, the air felt lighter. His hand made soothing strokes along her lower back, below her wing joints.

"Do you want to tell me what's wrong?" Oci asked, as if he didn't already know, as if he didn't know he was sent like the dark hand of the Fates to punish her. She sighed, letting her head slip to his shoulder, nuzzling into his neck. The Fates did have a cruel sense of irony, cursing her to love the man who was to be her downfall. And it was just that, she realized through the sickly haze, love. The floundering of her heart against her ribs as it beat itself against her chest, yearning to be free, to tie itself to his, could mean only that.

"No, no, I don't," she finally answered as she inhaled the thick smell of leather, whiskey, and salt from his skin. The smell did something to her; it curled up inside her and beckoned her, tempting her with dark desires.

She wanted to taste him, to savor him while she could, to wrap him in her soul and nurture their strange connection, but she didn't have the words, so instead, she pressed her lips against his skin. A hesitant brush followed by another, each bolder than the last, stacking atop one another until she pressed the last to the corner of his mouth.

Oci groaned, his hand fisted harder into her hair. "Safiya, you are unwell." The words were racked with vibrant desperation.

Safiya tilted her head, her words a whisper against his lips, daring him to give in, "Then be my tonic."

That was all the permission he needed. He rocked forward, pressing her back onto the cold stone, nailing her to the floor with a kiss so searing it could have birthed a new sun as she wrapped her legs around his hips.

He claimed her then, with such ferocious need and wanton abandon that tears pricked the corners of her eyes as he showed his truest self to her in a flickering moment of raw beauty. The wraps he'd kept so tightly on their bond slipped as they found their rapturous peaks together, and for a single heartbeat, she knew that she was his and he was hers until the stars died and the fragments turned to dust.

When they were done, splayed against the floor, Oci pulled her up and onto his chest, drawing her head into the protective hollow of his arms, his breaths still heaving.

After a pause to let their hearts slow, Safiya lifted her head to hover over his, letting her scarlet tresses spill around them as if that could hide them from the Fates. "Marry me, Oci. Be my king."

He went preternaturally still; his golden eyes searched her face for a lie. "You don't mean that." His words were rasped, pulled from him by a thread of disbelief.

She pressed a kiss like a coffin nail to his brow. "Oh, Oci, but I do."

Chapter 43

Safiya felt as though she'd accidentally Traveled to another Fragment that was one part fever dream, one part fairy tale. A halo spun around Oci's head as the priestess atop the Fates Spire inked their hands with the sacred matrimonial markings. But in her eyes, it was the quicksilver blood of the Fates themselves that was dabbed into their skin. The oaths they spoke did not stick in her mind after they were uttered, for the beauty in them was too pure for her addled mind to contain. Bliss ran through her veins in place of blood and love.

A contract was also produced, the first in history. It was one that must be signed in blood and witnessed by the priestess. It tied her and Oci together not only as man and wife but as king and queen. He was the first man in all Gypette to be more than just a consort or concubine to the queen. The Fates seemed to lean in to watch as the document was laid bare before them, their breaths held, the starlight pulsed with the beat of their hearts as they watched history being made. Without hesitation, Safiya pricked her finger with the nib of the quill and scratched her name across the parchment.

When she was finished, she offered the quill to her love, her husband, her executioner, and he took it, his face suddenly leeched of color, in fingers that shook. She smiled at him, the Honey crooking the corner of her mouth in an odd smirk. "Having second thoughts, my love?" *About the marriage, the kingship, the poisoning?*

He met her glassy-eyed gaze and whispered so only she and the listening Fates could hear, "Tell me again that you mean this, that this is what you want."

Safiya took a step closer and wrapped her hands around his. She drew the nib of the quill to the softly calloused pads of one of his fingers and pressed it until his blood blossomed. "I want this, Ocidynus. Even if you are to be my ruin, I will go with you gladly a smile on my lips and my love alight in my heart." She pressed a gentle kiss to the fluttering pulse of his neck before guiding his hand to sign his name next to hers sealing their destinies.

Chapter 44

Abrax watched as the cosmos smudged, like a hand swiped across a street urchin's chalk drawing, until it bled together in purple and blue swirls. The only thing that stayed in sharp relief was her. Moonlight glanced off her silver and gold feathers, illuminating her in a nebulous corona. Her wingtips stirred the stars and left them dancing in her wake as she twirled through the air. She swooped over to him, meeting him in the ether, her fingers tangled with his, her laugh musical on the wind as she pulled him into her orbit and into her wild dance.

Her pupils were blown so wide that her irises were naught but a slivered copper halo around the black. Their gazes crashed into one another. Something feral and as charged as a lightning strike passed unspoken between them.

Xandrina leaned in and brushed her lips like a tentative promise across his. Abrax's whole body went ridged. He caught her chin as she pulled back, her lips parted as if to say something, but he spoke before her words could fall between them.

"Don't toy with me, Princess, I am not one of your nobles' sons to be played with and then thrown aside. So if you're going to kiss me, you had better mean it." He let go of her chin and took her hand, slipping it through the open V of his jacket and shirt. He pressed her extended talons into his flesh hard enough that he felt small ruby droplets of blood bead along his skin. "My heart, Princess, beats only for you. I will stand at your back from now until the Fates' last breaths rattle through their chests and time ceases to exist; I will worship at your feet and dance with you among the stars; I will be yours wholly and completely. But if you don't want me, if you don't feel the same, then I beg you, have mercy and tear my heart out. Rip it from me and let me fall into the sea, but for the love of Fates, Princess, don't play games with me."

There was an agonizing pause before she wrenched her claws free and ran her bloody hand tenderly across his cheek. Silver tears pooled at the corner of her eyes and beaded like drops of morning dew along her lashes. Her lower lip quivered as words he never thought he would hear began to pour from them. "I will stand with you, Abrax, not ahead of you, I will be by your side wholly yours, body and soul without pretense. I will lay myself raw and bare before you because as much as I wish it didn't, as much as I want to deny it, my heart beats only for you."

Without warning, she ripped the barrier down around their bond, and all her emotions surged like sunlight into him, filling him with brilliant, effervescent feelings of adoration and love that chased away the haunted shadows of his past that curled in the corners of his mind, until he was overflowing with pure ecstasy. Abrax's emotions melded into hers before looping back into him, reminiscent of the push and pull of the tides. His lips crashed into hers in a kiss so all-consuming their wings forgot to beat, and they plunged from the heavens, cascading through the clouds. Free-falling.

Fingers tangled in hair as they tasted one another's confessions on their conjoined lips, the tender words hotter and headier than any amount of Honey could be. The sea reached up and wrapped them in her arms as they splashed down before she quickly heaved them onto a salt-stained shore gasping for breath and for the taste of one another. Laces were undone, sodden clothes were torn from skin that prickled with desire, the planes of which were hungrily tasted and explored. Their unspoken emotions coursed through their bond, knotting around one another and braiding their hearts together to beat as one.

As the first bleary streaks of dawn bruised the sky and the tide receded with the setting moon, Abrax broke their kiss and cradled Xandrina's face in the palm of his hand, his thumb sweeping along her jaw. She was it, the better life he had promised his mother on her deathbed that he would find, and even with his mind soaked in Honeyed sweetness, he knew she would be his home, his happy ending, until his heart ceased to beat. He pressed his forehead to hers and whispered words that would forever fail to encompass the depth of his feeling for her, but they would have to suffice until he could find better ones. "I love you, always and forever, Merjai."

Chapter 45

The sun crept over the horizon slowly as if it wished to give the sand and sea-soaked lovers more time to dress and sort themselves out. Xandrina felt as giddy as a feather on the wind still as she stole glances at the beautifully scarred expanse of Abrax's skin while trying to shimmy her way back into her skirt that was little more than torn ribbons at this point. Abrax caught her looking and grinned. "Something I can help you with, Princess?"

Her lips curled into a coy smile. "Well, now that you mention it, you could make yourself useful and lace up the back of my corset."

He laughed but stood, brushing the sand from his skin, and slid in place behind her and began tugging the ribbons at her back. She drew her hair over her shoulder. His breath, hot on the nape of her neck, brought back vivid flashes of the night before and sent the most pleasant shivers down her spin. "What does Merjai mean?" she asked him softly.

He slid his arms under her wings and wrapped them around her waist, folding her into him. "It's old valkry. It means beloved of my soul."

She tried the word out, tasting it on her tongue. It was sweet and tender, and more importantly, it felt right. He felt right.

She turned, placed her hands on either side of his face, and stared into the depths of his uniquely stunning eyes, so full of love for her. "I will love you, Merjai, until there is nothing left of me but the songs of mourning dancing across the sands. Through blood and ruin."

He pulled one of her palms to his lips and kissed it, then the other, and folded her hands in his, keeping them tucked against his chest. He leaned his head down, pressed his forehead to hers, and sighed. "We should be getting back, before someone wonders at our absence."

Xandrina didn't want to go back; she didn't want to leave this little sliver of sand that they had made their own. Going back meant facing what she had just done, the oaths she'd broken by laying with a man before magically producing a female heir. She could have her crown and title stripped for this. She didn't want to break this spell, but her next words would. Abrax slipped his fingers gently under her chin and tipped her face up to his. Worry creased his brow. "What is it, Merjai?"

She spat the words out half under her breath, as though that could soften the blow, as if that could make them any less true. "No one can know."

She couldn't look at him, she didn't want to see the hurt she was sure she would find in his eyes, but she could hear it anyway in the way he whispered, "I know." And it cleaved her heart in two.

Chapter 46

Oci looked out at the sea of faces before them, as grim as the grave and as ashen as the dead as they watched he and Safiya stand arm and arm. Neither spoke a word, they didn't have to, their inked declaration of matrimony plain upon their skin said it all.

Safiya's talons dimpled against his forearm. The courtiers around them rippled and shifted in the wake of two lone figures who entered the formal reception hall on the far side. Oci knew them without having to turn his head. The princess and the Mutt. He stuffed a growl that threatened to rise in his throat back down. If the two idiot children had been in the princess's chambers when he and Safiya had gone to give them the news, perhaps this whole thing could have been less of a spectacle. But even as they broke through the closest ring of nobles, Oci knew it was not them he was mad at but himself. His queen, his wife, was in no fit state to be out of bed, her shoulders shook with the strain of being upright, and her eyes were as glassy as a doll's. He should have pushed her harder to wait, but those fucking beasts in his head were circling, gnashing their teeth, demanding.

"Ah good, Xandrina." Safiya's voice sounded thin as it echoed around the all too silent room where not even a feather ruffled. "At last, Ocidynus and I have news."

Xandrina's wings bristled, her shoulders stiffening. "I can already see the news for myself, majesty." She spat the title in a way that made it seem more insult than formality. The hair on the back of Oci's neck stood on end at the insult.

"No, dear, that is not the whole of it." Ocidynus rooted his feet to the tiled floor and forced himself to breathe through his anger, as every sphynx in the room seemed to suck in a collective breath. "I have made Oci my king."

Ocidynus had expected to feel triumphant in that moment; he'd envisioned it a thousand times, if not more. They should have been in private council session when it was announced that he, the prince and heir of the fallen valkry kingdom, raised as a slave and as a soldier of Gypette, had managed to take the throne and conquer the conquerors when everyone assumed him dead, his bones long rotted into the soil. This was to be the day the blood of his family would be repaid in the ruin of their kingdom. He'd envisioned summoning the beasts to infiltrate the castle, the pandemonium that would ensue as he handed over the queen and the princess for them to take to their master, the blood on the floor as he walked across the corpses of the sycophantic idiotic simpering nobles who wouldn't bow to his rule. But here now in the moment, standing on the edge of everything he'd wanted, he couldn't make the final leap. He could not call the beasts to him.

The princess went as pale as the rest of them, a buzz of whispered words broke out and rushed like wildfire among the assembled as the news spread to the farthest reaches of the room. Xandrina's hand fluttered to her throat, the other braced on her bonded's arm. It was as discomposed as he'd ever seen her. Emotions warred on her face, and her lip quivered, caught between all the things he imagined she wanted to say, to scream.

"Perhaps we could speak in private, Princess," Oci offered, though fuck him if he knew what there was to talk about. This wasn't supposed to happen like this, but he couldn't seem to stop himself.

Her shrewd copper calm snapped back into place, and she let ice fill her words as she squared her shoulders. "Yes, I believe that would be best."

A small and strange part of him wanted to tell her he knew what she felt, what it was to lose the kingdom that was promised to you in the span of a few moments. But he silenced it and said nothing.

"After you." Safiya began to gesture to her daughter, but she wavered, her skin went suddenly waxy, her eyes rolled to the back of her head. Somewhere in the room a woman screamed as the queen began to fall.

Part
Three

Chapter 47

After Safiya so publicly fainted, the journey back passed in a haze of days spent traveling in a palanquin and nights spent in Ocidynus's arms, exploring one another's bodies with a feverish frenzied tenacity. A small part of her bled on the inside, splintered open by the not so small fact that he'd poisoned her to begin with. But since the time of their marriage, all her drinks were blissfully bitter or lacking in flavor at all. He'd ceased the Honey's flow, a vindication in her mind that his love for her was true.

The withdrawals were nearly as bad as the Honey itself, in some ways worse. Her mother's corpse was in every corner, in every shadow, whispering, muttering, screaming at her. But she was not the only hallucination that caught Safiya's eye, she saw imagined glances and clandestine touches between her daughter and her strange-eyed bonded, council members plotting rebellion and assassination, and strange creatures lurking around the edges of their camps.

Despite all the Honey withdrawals conjured before her eyes, the queen waved away every offer to attempt a magical healing from her daughter and cups of bitter herbs from the well-meaning apothecary. In her eyes, there was nothing to be done now but get home and see her new husband set upon the throne and her daughter safe. She did not want to give anyone false hope that they could do anything to prevent her demise. Even though the Honey had stopped flowing she could feel the imminence of her death in the way the stars peered at her each night and in the way she could feel the pull on the long-gone bond between her and Victrus. She would slip beyond the Veil willingly and glad that she'd at least found real and true love, even if it was only for a short while—that she'd done what was asked of her to save her daughter. That would soothe the ache of all that she had to atone for and all that she would leave undone and unmended.

She'd insisted on riding into Evernedi on horseback, she would be every inch the queen as she rode into the city with her king by her side. In bed the night before, she'd whispered her plans to announce him as her husband and king on the steps of the palace as soon as they'd finished their progress through the city.

The gates creaked open ahead of them, the streets were lined with people already waiting to greet them, but even before crossing the threshold, Safiya could tell something was not right. The wrongness of it beat alongside her heart, unsyncing it from its normal rhythm.

The clatter of the horses' hooves was the only sound as they rode in on the main road. The hateful and seemingly accusatory stares of the onlookers burned her already fevered skin. Their silence shredded like a thousand hot daggers through her soul until she thought she would weep. But she couldn't.

"Why do they say nothing?" she whispered brokenly, half to herself, though she knew Oci was close enough to hear.

"I don't know, but if I had to take a guess, I'd say that a fucking rat advisor, Fayden sent word ahead of our marriage."

She fought to keep her face smooth, serene, but venom and rancor filtered through the air and nettled against her skin, chafing. She was the crown, but the crown was the people, so what was she if the people turned on her?

Oci bridged the gap between them, nudging his horse closer so he could put a hand on her shoulder, the tips of his dark and leathery wings brushing against hers. Was it her imagination, or did a hiss whip through the crowd? Did they recoil, or did the streets simply widen, giving them a clearer path?

She looked over at Oci who was already looking at her with a stitch of worry sewn between his brows. He nodded as if he could read the unasked question in her eyes. He laced his fingers through hers, and as one, they shot from their saddles into the air, soaring over the discontented masses and headed straight for home.

She landed on the balcony with a wobble to her knees and to her lip. She barely made it two steps before she collapsed in a heap of feathers and tears. She knew this was what the Fates ordained, but it didn't make the echo of her heart shattering any less loud in her ringing ears.

Chapter 48

Abrax crouched against the palace wall, his back pressed into the stones as he sharpened his knife. Farther down the balcony, he watched Xandrina converse with the statue of Glendora with frantic finger-jerking movements. He caught glimpses of the words here and there. He tried to advert his eyes to give them privacy, but the worry that coursed through the bond that the princess had yet to reshield, and the anger, kept pulling his gaze.

Their conversation apparently over, Glendora slid away on surprisingly silent footsteps for one made of stone, far quieter at least than the princess's as she stalked over to him and threw herself down next to him. She let her head fall onto his shoulder, the spill of her copper hair a stark contrast against the black of his leather coat. "Glendora says she's sleeping, but that that bastard has barred entry, even to the statues." She heaved the words as if the burden of getting them off her chest was almost more than she could bear.

He set down his knife and stone and wrapped an arm around her shoulders, tucked her into the crook of his arm, and let her curl into him. He said nothing, knowing that she needed this moment to be vulnerable, to be small and scared and angry away from the eyes of apoplectic councilmen and riotously hurt citizens. She needed to lean on him the way so many leaned on her. Abrax stroked her hair, sending all the calming and loving feelings he could down the bond to chase away the shadows in her mind, just as she chased away the darkness from his with her mere presence.

Xandrina did not cry, but after many heartbeats of stillness, a shuddering sigh slipped from her lips, and she straightened from his hold. "Glendora told me the council has requested another meeting; we should get ready to attend."

Abrax nodded and stood, offering his hand to her and hoisting her to her feet when she took it. "Will he be there?"

She pressed a hand to his chest and looked up to meet his eyes. "I'm so sorry, Abrax. I forgot in all of this that he is your friend." There was genuine sorrow and remorse knitted into her words, and it hurt his heart in a new and wonderfully heavy sort of way that at a time such as this she was thinking of him at all when she had every right to be selfish.

He slipped his arms around the dip of her waist and pulled her flush against him and pressed his forehead to hers. "I keep thinking that, as unlikely as it is, that maybe he did fall in love with her as I did you Merjai."

She chuckled against him darkly before raising her hand to his face and pressing her palm to his cheek. "From your lips to the Fates' ears, Abrax."

Umbri is here. Lyrahvi's words hissed in warning to the both of them, if the way Xandrina jumped from the cradle of his arms, leaving him instantly hollow, was any indication.

A moment later, the petite sphynx, and Xandrina's new lady's maid brought home from the seaside, called for the princess to come in and dress. Abrax had the distinct feeling that Xandrina had saved her somehow, not that he knew the particulars. But it spoke to her deep love for her people that she would bring the broken woman here to heal and start anew, as if it was a perfectly natural and ordinary thing to do. That's why he loved her, though, because to her it was.

Xandrina looked over her shoulder before ducking inside, a silent question in her eyes, which he answered with a nod. He would be ready and waiting when she was done because whatever was coming next, they would face it together.

Abrax stooped to gather his knife, still on the ground, and when he stood, a mass of churning purple clouds caught his eye as it swept across the desert. A storm was coming—how fitting since there seemed to be one brewing within the walls of the keep as well. The Fates must have a sense of humor.

Chapter 49

The Mad Queen's face hovered over hers, though it was different than Safiya remembered. Her mother's mouth cracked into a wicked smile, ichor bleeding from gums that held crumbling and jagged teeth. She ran fingers that were more bone and sinew than flesh through Safiya's hair as she laughed softly.

Safiya whimpered, she wanted to call out for Ocidynus, to beg him to banish this phantom from her room, but the Honey withdrawals held her tongue in its firm and sticky grip, coating her mouth and throat with the ghost of its putrid sweetness. The only sound she could make was a wet and soggy rattling dredged from deep within her lungs.

"Hush now, daughter, don't try to speak, it will only make it worse." The ghoulish version of her mother cackled; her fingers moved to soothe over the scar across Safiya's lips. "Remember what I said about speaking out of turn."

A tear slipped down her cheek, carving a path through her fevered blush. She did remember. She was years younger than Xandrina was now when she made the rash and emotionally enflamed decision to stand against her mother's cruelty. Her mother didn't have to utter a single word of reproach, the crack of her whip against Safiya's face said it all and more. Safiya blinked the memory away and with it blessedly went the decaying image of her mother, but in its place stood her daughter. It was not the beautifully grown daughter she had now, but the young and broken version with the crumpled face sodden with the tears of confusion and hurt, calling out for her as she walked away, distancing herself for their safety.

Was this what death was meant to be? A procession of those whom you'd wronged come to see for themselves that Fate had in fact caught up with you at last? A blink later and the childish version of her princess was gone too, and Safiya was utterly alone.

Chapter 50

The voices whispered through Ocidynus's mind on a razor-tipped wind, circling him. Watching. He was the linchpin holding back the inevitable. On his signal, they would move, but he wasn't fool enough to believe such creatures would hold on his command for long. They were furious at his delays, but he just had to hold them off a little longer until he could get rid of the Honey, the last vial of it was in his pocket burning against his thigh, and figure a way out of this.

The glass-domed ceiling of the council chamber rattled with the first peel of thunder, but it was nearly drowned out by the shouts of seething councilmen.

Oci sat in the queen's chair at the head of the table, a move he knew did not go unnoticed, not by the council members and certainly not by the stoic steely gazed princess whose position he'd usurped with the stroke of a pen on his wedding night.

The council members pulled the document that named him as king and heir from each other's hands, like beasts snatching a mangled carcass from one another, to chew on what little morsels they could gnash from it. But nothing they found would satiate; there was nothing they could glom on to to knock him from the throne no matter how long they looked.

His head throbbed from keeping the circling creatures from his mind, and the added din of men arguing was doing him no favors where he slouched, leaning irreverently against his propped-up hand. He growled, partially out of pain and partially out of annoyance at these useless minions. They all fell silent. "I think that's fucking enough." He stood as their mouths fell, all save for the princess whose eyes bored into his as if she wished to scoop his brains from his skull to divine his truths.

She leaned in slightly as if what she had to say was meant for just the two of them and there wasn't a sea of saggy-sacked sphynx between them. "What illness is it that is plaguing my mother, majesty?" There was no sarcasm in the title she gave him or venom, but the way it landed still somehow made it perfectly clear what she thought of him. "I would like to see her— heal her if possible."

Magic glittered like a dark starry night at her fingertips, the stark opposite to the gilded version that dripped from Safiya's fingers. It was that magic that the creatures wanted the queen and the princess for, and it was the sight of that power that sent the beasts scurrying in a near feral mass in the back of his mind.

There was a screech in the distance that echoed in his subconscious, and the tether that tied the control he had over the creatures snapped like an old thread. He felt the blood drain from his face.

They were coming. The Fury were coming for his queen.

Chapter 51

Abrax watched with a grim face as Ocidynus stood from his chair so abruptly it went clattering violently back against the mosaiced floors and splintered into three pieces. He stomped from the room without a word of acknowledgment for what Xandrina asked. The council chamber erupted with agog shouts that careened around the walls and magnified. Xandrina nodded discreetly to Abrax, silently pleading for him to follow the now king. He slipped unnoticed from the council chambers as the princess stood and held her hands up to the rabble, and shouted, "Enough, gentle-sphynx, please."

He stalked out of the hall in the wake of Oci's near palpable fury. "Oci," he called, "Oci, wait!"

The black of the older man's cloak whipped around corners in a near run, but Abrax finally caught up to him in the hall by the royal rooms, stalling him with a hand on the shoulder. "Oci, I . . ."

Oci spun, startling a vial out of his hand. His red-rimmed eyes stared in wild panic as the fragile glass and cork bottle shattered on the floor outside of the queen's chamber door, and he swore in frustration.

"Shit. I'm so sorry, Oci. I was calling your name, here let me clean it up." Abrax pulled a handkerchief from the pocket of his trousers and began to kneel at the same time Oci growled, "Leave it for the servants, Mutt," and shoved him back from the mess.

But it was too late, the thick cloying scent of sickening near-rotted sweetness from the golden liquid materialized between them like a ghost. Abrax looked at the small puddle on the floor, his brow furrowed, and his mind reeled to reconcile all the pieces of what he knew and what was before him. Oci flinched as Abrax dipped a finger into the viscous liquid and touched it to his tongue.

He swallowed hard around a clotting lump of dread that filled his throat with the too familiar taste. "Honey. Oci, tell me this isn't what it looks like."

The older man glanced at the suite doors next to him as if contemplating making a break for it before he swiftly turned a furrowed glare on him. "Get lost, Mutt, you have no business here."

Fury hot and bright suddenly burst to life inside Abrax like a little sun come to set between his ribs. "Is this why the queen is sick, Oci? Are you poisoning her?" He stood, brandishing the finger he'd dipped in the Honey accusatorially in Oci's face.

He didn't want the words to be true, though even as he spoke them, the ashy sense of dread that filled his mouth told him they were.

Oci's lips curled, his eyes darkening, into a smile devoid of anything resembling the valkry he knew, the valkry he'd nearly died saving in the harpie raids. "No one will believe you, Mutt, you don't have any evidence." The words came out as a lethal growl dripping with dark, bloody, threats.

Abrax squared his shoulders and slid one foot back, bracing himself to fight or to run. "I have my word, and for the princess, that will be enough."

Oci lunged before Abrax could blink. One moment he was a few strides away, and the next he had Abrax pinned to the floor, straddling his chest, a hand clamped around his jaw. "She won't if you have no words to give."

Oci drew a lethal-looking blade from his boot and whittled it in a line along the seam of Abrax's lips. "I told you to leave it be, Mutt, you should have listened."

Abrax thrashed and bucked, but somehow the bigger man had his arms pinned, and the pressure of his knees on his wings when he jerked was unbearable. He tried to bite the king's fingers as he pried his mouth open. He tried to scream around them, but it came out garbled as the king took hold of his tongue.

There was a blinding pain so sharp he saw nothing but stars. He was choking on hot, thick metallic liquid as it filled his mouth and flooded the back of his throat. The sickening slap of meat against the floor had him turning his head to stare dazedly at the bloody lump of pink flesh that Oci threw down next to them. His vison reeled, blackening around the edges, splitting, and doubling, then merging again kaleidoscoping the gory image in a sick and grisly dance.

The crack of a palm across his face centered him for a brief moment, sharpening Oci's furious expression where it hung spattered in blood over him. "Do you have anything to say to me now, Mutt?"

Chapter 52

Xandrina slammed the door of the council chambers and heaved a sigh as she turned to head toward the gardens. Raining or not, she was in desperate need to clear the cobwebs of concern from her mind, and besides, her mother's balcony overlooked the lily garden. If Oci wouldn't let her see her mother, she would take matters into her own hands.

A small and weak part of her had been whispering in the deepest parts of her subconscious since the moment she discovered what her mother had done that perhaps this was a blessing. She had, after all, crossed lines with Abrax, more than once, lines that made it harder and harder each day to remember why she wanted to rule this country so badly. Yes, she loved her people, and she would do anything for them, but what if the best thing she could do for them was to just step aside and let her mother have her way? What if Abrax was right? What if she and Oci really were in love, and she was fighting against it?

A marble finger scraped across her shoulder, and the smell of lichen and crumbling stone dust that followed was one she knew well, Glendora. She turned to find the statue's fingers already moving so rapidly it was hard for her to catch what the long-dead queen was trying to say.

Wait, wait, slow . . . Pain sliced through the bond, white hot and so all-consuming it stole her breath. She doubled over. Her knees cracked against the ground.

Cold, unliving fingers slipped under her chin and tilted her tear-streaked face upward. Glendora's brow furrowed, her free hand dancing the words, *What is wrong, Princess?*

My bonded. She was barely able to twist her fingers to make the words, but Glendora seemed to understand all the same. The statue took off in the opposite direction, her steps thundering in the hall as the edges of Xandrina's vison spotted with dark stars.

The princess writhed on the floor, her fangs biting into her lip until blood welled from them to silence the scream that tried to claw its way up her throat. With a barely grasped force of will, she managed to submerge the bond in the deepest part of her mind, muting the pain to the pulse of a mild headache. She shoved herself to her feet, gulping down breaths, and threw herself in the direction Glendora had gone mere moments before.

Come, princess. To your rooms, your bonded is gravely injured. As Lyra's words lanced through her mind, she shifted direction, cold sluiced through her veins as she realized the Tatzelwurm had called both of them by their formal titles belying the severity of the situation.

Her heart kicked against her ribs as she used her wings to push herself along the corridor with as much speed as she could muster. *I'm coming.* She prayed to the Fates she wasn't too late.

Chapter 53

Oci watched as Safiya's fretting, fevered fingers plucked at the thin embroidered sheet that covered her. She whimpered. That small, weak sound called to him, pulled him by the heartstrings to her bedside where he knelt and soothed a scared and trembling hand over her brow.

With as much tenderness as he could summon, he brushed strands of scarlet hair from her forehead. He flinched as he realized blood still coated his fingers, Mutt—Abrax's blood. Safiya thrashed under his touch, battling against the sheets. "Oci," she cried through cracked and burning lips, "Oci, don't leave me." She twisted, grabbing his arm and dragging him closer.

"You are my dark vengeance," she whispered, as her eyes rolled into the back of her head, irises hiding beneath thick lashes, and then she was still.

Tears slid from Oci's eyes as he crawled into the bed with his queen and pulled her into his lap, cradling her. Her heart still beat, but it was thready and floundering. He held her head against his chest, letting his fingers fist into her tresses and rocked, whispering quietly into her hair. "Fates fuck me, what have I done?"

Lightning flashed through the slit in the curtained window, followed by the hammer of raindrops intent on being heard, on announcing the arrival of the beasts, of the Fury. He could feel them circling, taunting him. He'd made a deal in the dark, and they were here to collect whether he wanted them to or not.

Chapter 54

Abrax wasn't sure if the nauseating spiral of pain and dread that surged through him was his or if it was coming from his bond with the princess. He tried to open his eyes, unable to make sense of the disarrayed blur of light and color, then quickly shut them again. Something was terribly wrong, he knew that, but was there something wrong with him or someone else? And wasn't there something he had to tell Xandrina? Something important.

A hushed whisper in his ear muttered soothing words. He wanted to listen, to know what it was saying, but what little he could grasp seemed disordered.

A soothing darkness washed over his mind, stars winked in and out of existence, nebulas spun, all of creation lived and died in those celestial bodies.

You go to far, his body cannot take this kind of healing, neither can you, a voice hissed, though it sounded familiar, it also was too far away for him to care, not when the beauty of the heavens was laid out before him in his mind. There was just one thing missing, a vacancy opposite his consciousness that should be spinning in the night sky with him.

Then help me, Lyra! That tone, he knew it, knew it like he knew the beat of his heart. He tried again to open his eyes to see her face so he could remember her name.

"Abrax, come back to me." The words were so full of unmistakable command. A demand that pulled on something deep within and jerked his mind into waking. His eyes flung open, and with a gasp and in sharp relief above him leaned the most beautiful face he'd ever laid eyes on. The princess, his princess.

She pressed her forehead to his, her hands pressed to either side of his face, as tears fell from her copper eyes to stream down his cheeks. "Don't ever scare me like that again, Merjai," she whispered.

He let a hand come up and tangle in her hair. He opened his mouth to tell her he was fine, but only a croak came out.

With a jerk, he shoved her away and sat up. He tried again to speak and again, but there was nothing but garbled moans, and then he remembered, Oci, the knife, the Honey.

Xandrina was in front of him, making soothing noises and trying to grab his hands, insisting he calm down, but calm was so far behind him it wasn't even visible on the horizon. He charged to his feet, his wings unfurling behind him.

What are you trying to do, fool man? Lyrahvi snapped, her head poking from behind Xandrina's shoulder.

He groaned in exasperated relief. *Lyra, thank Fates, Oci is poisoning the queen.*

His bonded went unnaturally still as soon as he thought the words. The Tatzelwurm must have looped their thoughts together somehow.

What do you mean? Xandrina growled along their mental connection at the same time Lyra hissed, *show us what happened.*

Abrax closed his eyes, recalling the altercation with Oci in the hall in as vivid detail as he could while simultaneously pushing it toward the flickering connections he could feel in the depths of his mind. They took the memory like flame takes paper, wholly devouring.

A snarl cut through the room. Abrax opened his eyes to find Xandrina throwing open her weapons chest, sparks of magic spitting angrily from her fingers, floating around her before they fizzled and fell.

"I'm going to cut off that sneaking rat's head and stew his remains for the dogs." She growled as she began to pull sheaths and blades from the trunk.

Abrax ducked into his room and came back with a small arsenal of his own. When Xandrina saw him, she blanched, her fingers froze on the buckles of her breastplate. "What do you think you're doing?" Her eyes narrowed, glancing between all the places he'd strapped on weapons.

He smiled, though in his heart it felt more like a frown. He raised his hands and signed in that twisting finger language, *Through blood and ruin, Merjai.*

She shook her head. "No, I was barely able to heal you. You need rest. I can fight this battle."

Stop trying to protect me. I'm just the guard, remember? You're the princess. She swept across the room and caught his fingers up in hers.

You're not just a guard to me, Merjai. She spoke into his mind this time, the words echoed, leaving the impression of unshed tears and a heart bursting with love. Not since his mother had someone loved him. And never had he felt a love as pure and true and all-consuming as this, one that felt like the first rays of sun after the monsoon rains. He would not let her face a single day without him guarding her back, never mind letting her face Oci alone. He folded her into his arms, wrapping his black-feathered wings around them both in the useless hope that he could somehow shield them from any more heartbreak and harm.

Something is here. Lyra growled, her hackles rising from where she sat on the bed like a snake poised to strike, the claws of her purple-scaled paws elongated. *There is a presence.*

The princess's face darkened, and she shuddered beneath his hands. "I feel it too. It's all wrong. Like festering rot running its fingers along my magic."

Abrax dipped his chin. *Is there a way to reach the queen's chambers besides the balcony or door? I'm not sure what Oci is planning, but if this presence is his doing, we need to approach carefully.*

There's a passage, the doors have been sealed shut, but I think I can get them open. My mother used to use it to sneak into my rooms and tell me stories. Her eyes welled with tears, but there was a fierceness that burned them away before they could fall. *Come, it's in the closet.*

Xandrina's fingers shimmered as they shoved aside clothing and shoes to expose a seam in the wall. He didn't think he would ever tire of seeing her magic. With her wings painted in the luminous umber light radiating from her fingers, she looked like the ethereal Fate of Vengeance painted on the wall outside the garrison where his mother worked when he was small. If she was Vengeance, he would be her consort War.

The wall opened with her will, exposing a dank narrow length of ill-maintained hall. Xandrina looked over her shoulder at him and then at Lyra who slid across the floor, ready to go with them into whatever waited.

Xandrina turned and crouched before the Tatzelwurm, ruffling the sparse scruff of hair around her ears affectionately. "You can't come with us, friend." Lyra crossed her paws indignantly and hissed.

Something passed between them that they left him out of. Xandrina stood, and Lyra looked up at him, her eyes narrowed, weighted with determination. *Keep by her side, Snack, and get her out alive or I will eat you.*

He bowed his head, and by time he lifted it, the wurm was gone. *Where did you send her?* he signed to the princess as she drew her sword.

"She has her mission, and we have ours." She gave him a small, wicked smile that was all fangs and secret plots. "Ready for this, bonded?"

In answer, he drew his sword and stepped after her into the dark.

Chapter 55

Fear like he hadn't known since childhood raced along Oci's spine, as talons dragged along the glass, before burrowing into his skin to hide in his viscera. He'd been a predator so long he'd forgotten what it was like to be prey.

A face flashed in the panes of the window with the lightning, its maws hung loose, ichor bled from gums that held its serrated teeth, and then it was gone.

His mind spun as though it were as headily Honeyed as Safiya's had been. His breaths sawed against his ribs while his heart stood frozen and watched. His hair slipped from the knot at the back of his head as he turned his attentions back to the limp woman in his arms. He had to know, he had to know now before it was too late.

"Look at me, Saf, look at me." Her eyelids fluttered as he turned her face to his with a hand on her chin, her skin too hot beneath the pads of his fingers. "Good, girl. Now, no more games, love, no more lies. Tell me right now if it was real, if your love was real. If it was, I will burn this world for you. I'll burn it all down for you. I just need to know, was it real?"

Her eyes rolled to his, rimmed with Honey-gold tears, and her hand fluttered to his face, trembling like a dying bird. "It was real, Oci, of course it was real. I knew, all along I knew about the Honey. But I know"—she swallowed, thickly—"I know the Fates didn't allow you another choice. But you must know I love you now, and I'll love you, Erron Ocidynus Althorn, until my last breaths, and I'll find you again in the next life with my first."

The sound of his name, his true name on her lips speared him through the heart. Oci pressed a kiss to her forehead, then to her lips, and she kissed him back with everything she had as the sound of splintering glass in the sitting room sang above the sounds of the storm. He pulled reluctantly from their embrace, setting her to rest back against the pillows, and he stood, drawing his sword from where it leaned against the nightstand and turned to face the Fury that stalked around the shadowed corners of the room cinching him in.

"You cannot fucking have her." A growl tore from his throat more beastly sounding than even the creatures standing before them with their lethal talons and too-sharp faces.

Ocidynus raised his sword. The shattered light from the storm outside illuminated the swarming Fury in bits and pieces, hiding their true number and their movements, but he could feel their hollow, dead-eyed gazes perusing his stance, looking for a weakness.

"You made a deal with the Darkness Prince of the fallen kingdom." The words cracked like the bones of nameless conquered under the unfeeling boots of the vanquishers in unison around the dark room. "We have come to collect the two strongest travelers as was promised in return for the crown of this land."

"You gave me nothing," Oci spat, his hands white knuckled on the hilt of his sword as his eyes tried to trace their words, to mark where his quarry stood.

"You speak falsely, valkry, the Darkness gave you your plan, it crooned it to you deep within the mines. While you toiled, it sang to you of the sweet vengeance it could give. You cannot renege now just because you've discovered the taste of your revenge is bitter. You will give us the Traveler queen and her heir so we may bleed them."

"If it's blood that you want, then it is blood you shall have," Oci roared, and lunged toward the nearest creature, slashing with the sort of precision that could only be honed in the crucible of war. The thunk of a head hitting the carpeted floor of the room sent the Fury into a frenzy of gnashing teeth and ripping claws.

Suddenly light behind him flared, and he spun, turning his back on his enemy as he never had before to see Safiya as radiant as the dawn, her hands alight, brighter than the sun itself. She sent a bolt of pure golden cosmic fire toward the beasts nearest her with a wild scream that Oci felt echo around his soul.

"Mother!" A shout pulled his attention from his beloved as the princess of all people came charging from the queen's closet followed by the Mutt. Their frantic eyes jumped from the queen to him, their gazes crashing into his, filled with so many promises of death. For a long drawn-out heartbeat, they stared at one another, and Oci had the faintest hope that they would let him explain, but he realized it was too fucking late for that.

Xandrina lunged, but so too did the Fury, taking advantage of his distraction, for the queen. "No!" He swatted the princess away as if she was no more than a pest in his ear, but then there was Abrax blocking his path to the queen who struggled feebly between two Fury, her magic sparking and nearly spent at her talon tips.

Lightning struck the bed chamber window, obliterating it. The wind from the storm charged in, pelting them all with glass shards and rain. The two Fury holding the queen took advantage of the confusion, as Oci blinked blood from his eyes, and dove through the opening.

"Safiya!" Oci tried to throw himself off the precipice after her, but Xandrina and Abrax were again in his fucking way. Oci grabbed for the Mutt's wings to tear him off the sill so he could jump, but just then hands the felt like death upon him wrapped around his waist and pulled.

There was a horrifying squelch of ripping sinew and flesh. Blood sprayed the night-dark air around him, coating him, worming its way into his nostrils and between his lips. There was a scream and a blinding flash of nebulous magic that seared his eyes. When the spots cleared, he saw the princess dive over the sill of the window, disappearing from his line of sight, and in his hands hung the limp and ravaged bloody stumps of Abrax's wings.

What the fuck had he done? He heard that wall within him that separated valkry from mere beast fracture, break, and turn to dust. He dropped the torn appendages with a feral yell and with impossible strength summoned from the depths of his rage and despair, he writhed around in the Fury's grip and ripped its head from its neck. The body attached to the arms that caged him crumpled to the ground, and he spun using the mangled head in his hand to bludgeon the face of the foe that came at him next. Ichor spurted from its nose and mouth in thick black rivulets as he bashed it in again and again until he heard bone crack, and the Fury went as still as the first. He picked up his sword where it was discarded in the confusion and cleaved the next attacker in half. They would pay. They would all pay if he had to spend the rest of his life wiping them from existence. He would somehow find a fucking way.

The sound of wood splintering briefly caught his attention, and through the doorway to the sitting room Oci caught a glimpse between the seething mass of Fury, of stone figures marching with carved marble swords and the faintest glint of reflected lightning along the purple scales of what could only be the princess's pet.

Fucking great, more things that wanted to kill him. A voice that he supposed was his conscience whispered to him in the back of his thoughts that he didn't not deserve it.

Chapter 56

Xandrina tore after Abrax's limp body as it plunged through the rain toward the ground. She tucked her wings, her arms outstretched before her as she screamed for all the Fates to hear.

She pulled on their bond mentally, as if it could reel him back to her.

Her talons shot out of her fingertips, elongating to give her that extra inch to cover that fractional distance between her and her bonded, her Merjai. She swiped and missed. She tried again; her claws scratched against the torn leather slits of his jacket where his wings should be. Blood spun out of the gaping wounds, seeping into the rain around them, merging with the drops and painting them rust colored so all the air around her was tainted with the scent of his life leaking from him.

She roared in frustration. The ground was rising up to meet them quickly, too quickly. The wind filled her ears with its cries as she surged forward again grappling wildly for any purchase on Abrax's back.

Xandrina nearly sobbed with relief as the points of her claws pierced the thick back of his coat. She held on for all she was worth as she back beat her wings, fighting against his weight and the crushing wind.

The ground drew back. Lightning singed the air with the smell of ozone. She half flew, half dragged Abrax over the palace wall, left horrifyingly vacant of guards. Likely not a coincidence, she realized, as she flew sluggishly past a warped and cracked guard tower door.

In her arms, which were aching from holding his weight, Abrax whimpered. The sound was thin, barely audible as it twined its way to her ears. A fresh surge of anger and worry spurned her on as her wings thrashed wildly against the storm to carry them out over the city. She had to get them someplace safe, someplace warm, dry, and hidden where she could heal Abrax or at the very least staunch his bleeding.

Her feet slipped from under her as they landed somewhere in the Pit. Her tailbone jarred against the cobbled stones, forcing her to bite back a cry of pain as she fought not to let Abrax slip from her hold or let his head crack against the ground.

Mist crawled along the empty streets and up the walls of buildings to peer beneath lintels into windows. Xandrina shuddered as she shoved her sodden hair off her face. If the storm felt wrong before, it was ten times worse now.

Abrax muttered indecipherably, and his eyes flicked back and forth beneath his lids as if he were trapped in a nightmare, which wasn't far from the truth.

Xandrina grunted as she tried to haul Abrax's unconscious body up from where he was strewn across her so they could move. Spots dappled around the corners of her eyes, and her vision slid. A pain lanced through her side, sharp and hot in contrast to the cold that soaked through her clothes and the rain that dripped through the cracks in her breastplate.

She craned her neck to look back up at the palace, rain cut through the light from its windows, but she swore she saw the walls crawling with the sickening beasts she'd known only as legends in books until coming face-to-face with them. She wondered if Lyra had been successful in her mission, if she was alive, and before she could wonder or worry any more, she slipped into a fitful unconsciousness.

Chapter 57

The knife in Oci's hand bit into his throat. Pale-skinned corpses and the rubble of statues littered the floor of the throne room. How the fuck they'd fought their way there he didn't know, it was all a bloody blur. The knife had bought him a moment's pause as the Fury eyed it with cruel calculation.

His breath rattled against and clung to his ribs and failed to bring him any relief.

"You still owe us, valkry, the debt is not yet fulfilled." The Fury's voice raked against his eardrums like steel nails against stone. "The princess, we must have her, she holds great power."

Oci backed away as they stalked closer until the backs of his thighs hit the edge of Safiya's throne. "Give me back my queen and I'll do whatever you want." Fuck him, he'd never begged for anything in his life, but he would beg for her.

The Fury who'd spoken spat at the foot of the dais. "There is no going back on what was promised. It is too late for that."

As if the beast had planned it, as if it knew, the bond between he and Safiya went as silent as the grave. His knees buckled, and he slumped back onto the throne as the pain of her sharp and stark absence coursed through his veins. His soul was on fire. He screamed raw, and guttural, as he drove the knife into his neck. He could not leave her to greet the Fates on her own, he would meet her there, and they would walk hand in hand through the Veil and into the next life, a happier life.

With what little strength he had left to muster, he wrenched the knife free and let his blood flow. The Fury around him screamed, but he could not hear it over his gurgling laugher that echoed in his ears. He'd bested the bastards at least. The princess was smart; they would not have her. If there was one thing Safiya would want from him, it would be this, to save her daughter. At least he could do this.

The Fury stalked forward as blood began to pool in his lap as the room around him began to warp and fade. It grabbed him by his chin, bending down to lock its sunken eyes on his searchingly. "You think you've won, don't you?"

Oci's heart skipped a beat as the Fury's lipless face split into something akin to a malevolent grin. "You think you can best the Darkness?" It threw back its head and laughed. "It does not need your heart still beating to use you, valkry. Even in death, you are beholden to your promises."

The only King of Gypette, the heir of the fallen valkry kingdom, drew his last breath and spat in the Fury's face before his broken heart finally stopped beating.

Chapter 58

Xandrina knelt atop the swollen scarlet dune. Evernedi was naught but a spindled speck on the horizon shrouded in a storm that did not seem to want to let it out of its grasp. The setting sun cast the sky in violent shades of pink that bled into the coming night.

She and Abrax had barely managed to make it out of the capital alive. If it were not for the Fates of Luck and Fortune smiling upon them, they would have been dead before morning. As it was by some stroke of divine intervention, they'd landed on the stoop of the one person in the whole of the city who was the most likely to help them. The Mother of the foundling house. She took them in, tending to their wounds until Xandrina was strong enough to heal Abrax. She helped smuggle them out of the city as well, but not before word came to them of the king's proclamation, that she and her mother were dead. Mother risked much in helping them, but she doled out her kindnesses without ruffling a single feather.

There was still no word of Lyra, but Xandrina could feel her purring presence tucked safely in the back of her mind even at this distance. The Tatzelwurm at least was unharmed and, the princess knew, clever enough to be hiding.

Abrax knelt beside her and put a hand tenderly on her shoulder. She longed to nuzzle into it, to lean into his solid presence and weep. For her mother, for her kingdom, for him, for herself. But now was not the time for such weakness.

She raised her hands to the night sky and instead began to sing her mournful prayers to the Fates, the drawn-out words dredged from the depths of her soul. As she uttered the last notes of longing and grief, her heart shredded at the realization that life was nothing more than an echo across the sands.

When at last their shadows were drawn long across the sands pigmented purple in the sliver of moonlight cresting over the distant Pyramid Mountains, Abrax offered Xandrina his hand. She took it, allowing him to pull her to her feet and into the surety of his embrace. He was the rock against which she could brace herself to face anything.

He pulled a hand away to sign, *Where to next, Princess?*

She sighed weightily. "There is a monastery across the desert, a sequestered Order who will give us refuge. There we can hone our grief into rage to slit the throats of those who wronged us. We will find my mother if there is anything left of her to be found, take back our kingdom, and then you and I, Abrax, we will live. We will live to be so old that this will be nothing but a distant memory not worth recollecting."

He soothed a hand down her hair as he hummed his agreement, then together they turned hand in hand to walk across the desert toward the rising moon.

Continued in
The Songs That
Beckon

Their grief binds them.
The Song calls them.

The Darkness wants to claim them.

As winter wraps Areth in its frozen embrace, nightmarish beasts descend upon the Hastings household kidnapping Mr. and Mrs. Hastings and leaving behind their daughter, Bianca, as sole witness. In the wake of their abduction her quiet world is turned upside down and shaken revealing the secrets and lies her parents have buried.

As truths unravel it binds her to those who have similarly lost. Together they must wade through the thorny tangles of growing love and grief to find those that they hold dear before the looming threat of darkness is unleashed to destroy them all.

Praise for The Songs That Beckon

"The Songs That Beckon is an ethereal tale of loss, the struggle to heal, and hold onto hope while forging new connections, discovering magic and the adventures that show you who you are."
-H. Reynolds

"The Songs That Beckon is a dark yet whimsical tale that will transport readers to new worlds. With elegant prose that evokes visceral reactions, M.A. Brown has crafted a hauntingly beautiful story of love and loss."
– Stephanie Combs, co-author of The Stars Would Curse Us **@stephdevourerofbooks**

"A story of grief, grit, and adventure, told in a vivid and unique style that will pull you into a world unlike any you've known before."
-Beth Steadman **@bethstedman**

"The Songs That Beckon is an epic blend of gothic elegance, portal fantasy, and pining looks. If you have yet to read anything by M.A. Brown, treat yourself to her stunning storytelling and get lost in this immersive tale of navigating grief and love"
-Cynthia Brubaker, Author of the Gomada Academy Series, **@cb.novelist**

M.A. Brown is a stay-at-homeschooling mom living in Colorado with her husband and four kids. She loves to write fantasy with a healthy dose of romance, dreamy worlds, and a whole lot of magic. When she's not creating, she enjoys hiking, camping, and gardening with her family.

Follow her @writer.m.a.brown or find her on her website www.mabrownauthor.com.

X andrina came in to being by storm one random September day while I was dress shopping with my mom. I could suddenly see her so clearly. As soon as I got home, I immediately started outlining her and the world she came from. One thing I completely missed however were her feelings for Abrax. We all have Beth Stedmen to thank for their romance because for some reason I had it in my head that they were just REALLY good friends but then I realized they were in fact just hiding their relationship, sometimes even from themselves.

Safiya and Oci's story came a bit later, after I'd already started drafting Echo and suddenly the short story I was writing to flesh out a side character became a full blown tragically romantic novella. I spent many hours crying while writing scenes, laughing at their banter, and having mental break downs while I stressed over whether or not this story was any good. So many people got me through it who deserve all the thanks and the credit in the world, my kids and husband of course for putting up with me while I threw myself at this story like my life depended on it and suffered through a lot of crappy dinners and an erratic laundry schedule. Thank you, Stephanie, for reading my horrendously chaotic alpha draft and for making me feel like maybe it wasn't half bad after all. Thank you to Beth, not only for making me realize Xan and Abrax were in love but for helping me to make this story the best it could possibly be. And thank you to Chrissy, I'm sorry, I know my spelling and grammar are atrocious, you made this book readable and for that I am eternally grateful. To Heather, you're my hero for reading this whole thing in a weekend for me when I was on a deadline.

Thank you to all my amazing artists, if you haven't noticed already, bookish art is one of my all-time favorite things. To Maggie and Kaja my Cover and Undercover artists, you are both the kindest humans ever! Thank you for devoting your time to make Echo such a stunning and gorgeous book. To Lesya, your art literally made me cry when I saw it. Nirav, you are just the sweetest reader and artist, I adore every piece you do. And lastly, to Ashes, your sketches bring this story to life for that I am so very grateful.

A huge thank you to all of you, my readers, I appreciate each and every one of you for taking a chance on a baby author like me.

And last but never least, as always, thank you God for gifting me the crazy chaos that is my brain so that I can spin people and worlds into existence to put on the page.

If you enjoyed Echo Across the Sands, please consider leaving a review on Goodreads, Amazon or on social media, then check out some more books by Midnight Tide Publishing.
Thank you for reading.

The Iris were sent to us from the stars, but their rule is controlling and oppressive. Every season, we send our brothers and sisters to the marriage drafts . . . but the selected never return.

Aella - My world falls apart when my best friend and I are drafted to compete for the hand of Esterra's most eligible bachelor, the devastatingly handsome Iris prince. As an elemental fae, it should be the greatest honor, but the competition is filled with violence.

I question my true purpose as we fight to survive in games rigged against us.

Arianwen - Life should be simple—go on my rite and return to marry a man I've never met—but when a handsome stranger falls from the sky, everything is turned upside down. Secrets and lies unravel, leading me to question everything as I find myself pulled into a rebellion. My heart longs for a better world, but am I willing to forsake duty in pursuit of it?

We both face choices:

LOVE or DUTY

LOYALTY or ADVENTURE

FIGHT or SURRENDER

Is fate truly written in the stars, or have they abandoned us?

The Stars Couldn't Break Us is a fantasy romance novella set in world of The Stars Would Curse Us and should be read after Book 1.

Two lost hearts, an arranged marriage, and more than a social divide between them.

Can he survive the loss of his mate and open his heart to someone new?

Can she let go of her past and break through the walls he put up to keep her out?

Return to Iveria in this emotional and heartwarming installment in The Stars Would Curse Us series.